FLOWERS FOR THE GOD OF LOVE

For a moment they looked at each other. Then Rex said:

"I am afraid of telling you what is in my heart."

Because his voice was very soft and gentle Quenella felt herself tremble.

"You need not ... be afraid."

She was not sure whether she took a step towards him or that his arms drew her near. She only knew she was close against him, her heart throbbing wildly.

"I touched your lips once in gratitude," Rex said in a deep voice. "Now I want to kiss you for another reason."

But he did not kiss her. Instead he ran his fingers along the outline of her chin, downwards to her neck. It was a sensation she had never known, tingling like flames through her body.

"You are so beautiful," he exclaimed.

Then he looked into her eyes and his lips fell on hers. As they kissed it was impossible to deny the passion, the urgency, the all-consuming desire ...

They were reunited, but as the flames leapt higher and higher it was impossible to think, to speak, only to feel ...

Bantam Books by Barbara Cartland
Ask your bookseller for the books you have missed

Barbara Cartland
Flowers for the God of Love

BANTAM BOOKS · TORONTO · NEW YORK · LONDON

FLOWERS FOR THE GOD OF LOVE
A Bantam Book | July 1979

PRINTING HISTORY
E. P. Dutton edition published February 1979
Bantam edition | July 1979

ISBN 0–553–12281–9

Published simultaneously in the United States and Canada

*Bantam Books are published by Bantam Books, Inc. Its trade-
mark, consisting of the words "Bantam Books" and the por-
trayal of a bantam, is Registered in U.S. Patent and Trademark
Office and in other countries. Marca Registrada. Bantam
Books, Inc., 666 Fifth Avenue, New York, New York 10019.*

AUTHOR'S NOTE

The descriptions of the Viceroy's Palace in Calcutta, the Government Houses in Lucknow and Niani Tal, and the ceremonial protocol are all accurate. The true story of "The Great Game" has yet to be told in detail. It unexpectedly ended in 1903 when it seemed there was no way short of another mobilisation of the Northwest Frontier to keep Russian arms out of Kabul and just conceivably Peshawar.

Then, without warning, the crisis began to ebb as Russia suffered defeats by the Japanese Army and Navy, coupled with Anglo-Japanese Treaties in 1902 and 1905 which shifted the Asiatic balance of power heavily in Britain's favour.

At long last in an agreement signed in St. Petersburg in 1907 Russia recognised Afghanistan as a British sphere of influence.

But why? The answer lay in Germany's swift rise, on Russia's western border, to a world power.

It was in fact the fear of German military might that ended "The Great Game."

In 1903 Colonel Francis Younghusband headed a military mission into Tibet and reached Lhasa.

st professional—and he wondered whether it was
the pupil showing off what she had learnt or somet-
... which was flecked with her ...

... O'Garry, as if she had been well rehearsed,
... her feet.

"You must forgive me, Major Daniel, if I retire

Chapter One

1900

The hackney-carriage drew up outside the India Office and a man with a sun-bronzed face got out and paid the driver.

As he walked up the steps he found the door open, and a young man who looked the exact prototype of a budding diplomat hurried forward with outstretched hands.

"Welcome home, Major Daviot!" he said. "The Chief is waiting for you, and, I may add, impatiently!"

He smiled as he spoke and there was no mistaking the look of admiration in his eyes.

"It is very nice to be back," Rex Daviot replied.

They walked along the wide corridors embellished with pictures of Governors-General, emblems of Indian rivers and cities, and various types of Imperial Statuary.

The India Office was not clubbable. It was old, powerful, and sombre. It moved at a slow, despotic pace.

With its huge Library, its immense accumulated experience, it knew more about India than any other Government Office anywhere had ever known about another country.

1

"What was India like when you left?" the young man asked.

"Very hot!" Rex Daviot replied with a smile which prevented the words from sounding sarcastic.

"We are all buzzing with curiosity about your latest exploit."

"I hope not!"

"You must realise, Major, that it is impossible to stop people from speculating, even if they have very little to go on. I assure you we have done our best to keep everything very secret."

"I hope so," Rex Daviot remarked drily.

He knew even as he spoke that secrets had a mysterious way of leaking out in unexpected places, and in India the people in the Bazaars were usually aware of what was occurring long before the Commander-in-Chief had the slightest idea of it.

They reached a pair of impressive mahogany doors, and the young man opened them to say with almost a note of triumph in his voice:

"Major Rex Daviot, Sir!"

At the end of a very large room a man was sitting at a desk.

He rose, with an expression of pleasure on his face, and as Rex Daviot entered he came forward to greet him.

They met in the centre of the room, and Sir Terence O'Kerry, Head of the India Office, clasped the younger man's hand to say:

"Thank God you are home safely! I was afraid that something might prevent it."

Rex Daviot laughed.

"What you are really saying is that you are surprised I was not assassinated or my disguise was not penetrated."

"Exactly!" Sir Terence agreed.

"There were some uncomfortable moments, I admit

that," Rex Daviot said, "but here I am, safe and sound. You received my report?"

"I found it unbelievable, and so absorbing that I thought I was reading the kind of adventure-story I enjoyed as a boy."

"I am glad it pleased you," Rex Daviot said with a twinkle in his eyes.

They were dark grey eyes, a colour which he had found extremely useful when eyes of another colour might easily have betrayed him.

"I have quite a lot to say to you," Sir Terence said. "Sit down, Rex, and let me start from the beginning."

Rex Daviot looked slightly surprised, but he obeyed, seating himself in one of the green leather arm-chairs which flanked the mantelpiece.

Sir Terence sat down opposite and said in a serious tone:

"I do not need to tell you how grateful we are, and that your findings on this last mission will have very far-reaching repercussions."

"I hope you have been careful to discuss it with as few people as possible," Rex Daviot said. "I want to go back, and even the sand in India has ears!"

"You have already taken part in so many exploits that you cannot expect people not to look upon you as a kind of hero."

"I hope they do nothing of the sort!"

"Well, the Queen for one is ecstatic at what you have accomplished."

"Her Majesty is very kind; but quite frankly, I want to return as soon as possible and get on with the job. There is still a lot to be done."

"No-one knows that better than I do," Sir Terence replied, "but we have at the moment other plans for you."

A quick frown appeared on Rex Daviot's sun-

tanned forehead and for a moment his grey eyes
seemed to turn to steel.

"Other plans?" he questioned.

"That is what I want to talk to you about."

"I am listening, but I hope they will not prevent me
from returning to the Northwest Frontier."

"They will not do that, but you may go there in a
different capacity."

"What do you mean by that?"

"The Queen wants to appoint you Lieutenant-
Governor of the Northwest Provinces!"

Sir Terence spoke quietly, but the effect on the man
sitting opposite was almost as if a bomb had exploded
at his feet.

"Lieutenant-Governor?" he repeated, with a look of
incredulity on his face.

"Her Majesty feels that is now your rightful place,
and I agree with her."

"Why? Why?"

"Because you know as well as I do that you cannot
go on forever risking your life and not paying the pen-
alty. Your success has been fantastic to date, but . . ."

"I should have thought," Rex Daviot interrupted,
"that that would constitute a very good reason for me
to continue as I am now."

"I may tell you," Sir Terence said, "that this appointment has the approval of the Viceroy."

"I should have thought that he, of all people, would
have opposed a change, for the simple reason that I
make things very much easier for his Administration
than they would be otherwise."

"He is aware of that; but at the same time, the position of Lieutenant-Governor has fallen vacant in
somewhat tragic circumstances."

Rex Daviot was silent.

He knew what those tragic circumstances were and

he knew too that by being offered the position he could not have been paid a greater compliment.

At the same time, something within him rebelled against the formality, the protocol, and perhaps too the authority that such a post would carry.

No-one knew better than he did how important it was to have the right type of man in Government House at a time when unrest on the borders of India was growing and the tribesmen were being incited continually and sometimes successfully by the Russians.

Although on his way home he had wondered who would be appointed to the Northwest Provinces, he had never for one moment suspected that it might be himself.

Now as he was silent Sir Terence said:

"I should add that if you accept the position, Her Majesty intends to make you a Peer."

"A Peer? For Heaven's sake—why?"

"For a number of reasons," Sir Terence replied with a smile, "but first of all because in any other circumstances you would have received a high military award for this last expedition. But that would only draw attention to you, which I know is the last thing you want."

He paused before adding:

"It is usual for the Lieutenant-Governor to be titled, and as you know, the last six have been either knights or Baronets."

"But—why a Peer?" Rex Daviot enquired.

"Her Majesty wished to show her appreciation, and we could none of us think of a better way."

"You make me embarrassed!"

"It is not often that I say this to a man in this room," Sir Terence went on, "but you have not only been magnificent, you have also saved the lives of hundreds if not thousands of men who otherwise would have been ambushed and killed mercilessly in a way which does not bear thinking about."

Sir Terence and Rex Daviot both knew that the tribesmen on the Northwest Frontier did not allow their victims to die quickly.

The tortures and mutilations they inflicted on their prisoners would make the most hardened soldier vomit when he saw their bodies.

As if Rex Daviot found it easier to think on his feet, he rose from the chair in which he had been sitting to walk to the window.

He looked out, but he did not see the grey roofs, the trees in St. James's Park, or the busy traffic.

Instead, he saw bleak barren rocks behind which there might be a tribesmen with a gun, or, just as dangerous, a sharp pointed knife which could be thrust into a man's body without a second's warning.

The Northwest Frontier was one of the most legendary places on earth. No comparable area had seen so much bloodshed, intrigue, gallantry, savagery, patience, or sacrifice.

There was silence before he said aloud:

"Will you convey my deepest respects and gratitude to Her Majesty and tell her that while I deeply appreciate the honour she would confer on me, I must refuse it."

"Refuse it?" Sir Terence repeated. "Will you give me a reason?"

"For your own ear it is quite simple," Rex Daviot answered. "I cannot afford it!"

Again there was silence, for both of them knew that the important positions in India, from the Viceroy downwards, were all a tremendous drain on a man's private purse.

The Viceroyalty cost its incumbent so much money that no-one was able to accept it without a private fortune of his own.

The same applied to the other great positions in the land, those of the Governors of Madras and Bombay, the Lieutenant-Governor of the Northwest Provinces, and the Ruler of the Punjab.

The Resident of Hyderabad was on a slightly lower scale, but even he had to augment the official salary, which in every case was not enough for the amount of entertaining and the state in which Government Representatives were obliged to live.

"As it happens," Rex Daviot said, "I have had some considerable expense to bear in my family, which has increased my bank overdraft to what I imagine must be the limit! So I will just remain as I am."

There was no regret in his voice, and Sir Terence knew that Rex's astute and brilliant brain would have sized up the whole situation in the few minutes in which he had been looking out the window.

Having made his decision, he had set it to one side and would have no regrets.

"I had a feeling that that is what you would say," Sir Terence said after a moment.

Rex Daviot turned round with a smile.

"You have known me for at least ten years, Sir, so you know as much as I do about my private affairs."

They were both referring to the fact that Rex Daviot's father, before he had had a fall out hunting which had left him a semi-invalid, had run through the bulk of the family fortune.

It had left his only son and heir in the position where he had to rely entirely on his own resourcefulness.

Sir Harold Daviot had been born in the wrong century. He should have lived in the Georgian era, when a Buck was expected to be raffish and extravagant.

Sir Harold's mode of living under Queen Victoria earned him the label of being eccentric and caused

the more respectable members of Society to close their
doors to him.

Rex Daviot was himself a throw-back to his great-
great-grandfather, who, an outstanding and magnificent soldier, had been a General in the Bengal
Lancers at the time of Clive.

When Sir Harold had been stricken down and
forced into a wheel-chair, his son had quite quietly
taken on the tasks of paying off his debts and of im-
proving the family estate in Northumberland, which
had been sadly neglected.

He also found that he had to provide for a number
of ladies on whom his father had bestowed his favours,
only to leave them, after he tired of them, with his children and invariably penniless.

This was bad enough, but there were also the ever-
mounting medical expenses to be found, and because
he was immobile and had little to do, Sir Harold had
taken to gambling on race-horses in a way that he
could certainly not afford.

Sir Terence was aware how uncomplainingly and
good-humouredly Rex Daviot had shouldered a bur-
den which would have appalled a man of weaker
character and less sensibility.

Aloud he said:

"You know I understand and sympathise, and that
is why I have a suggestion to put to you."

"Another job?" Rex Daviot asked.

"Not exactly," Sir Terence replied. "But in fact it
concerns the one you have just refused."

"In what way?"

"That is what I am going to tell you."

Because he knew it was expected of him, Rex
Daviot walked from the window back to the chair in
which he had been sitting.

"A cigarette or a cigar?" Sir Terence offered as he
sat down.

Rex Daviot shook his head.

"Neither, thank you. I gave up smoking a long time ago. Indians have an acute sense of smell and the fragrance of an expensive Havana on a bearer or a rickshaw boy would definitely be suspect."

Sir Terence laughed.

"Are those your favourite disguises?"

"No. The East is notable for its Fakirs, and I cannot tell you how many ineffective prayers and curses I know in a dozen different dialects."

They both laughed, and, as if the sound eased the tension, Rex Daviot leant back to say:

"Tell me your second suggestion."

"It originally came from Her Majesty," Sir Terence replied. "While she is extremely anxious for you to take the post suggested, she asked me to tell you that she considers it essential that the Lieutenant-Governor of the Northwest Provinces should be a married man!"

For a moment Rex Daviot stared in surprise at the man opposite him. Then he said decisively:

"Well, that lets me out! I have not yet accepted the bonds of holy matrimony and I have no intention of doing so!"

"Why not?" Sir Terence enquired.

"The answer is simple. No woman would put up with my way of life as it has been up until now, and I have never met one with whom I wished to share the future."

"I am quite certain there have been many applicants for the job," Sir Terence remarked drily.

"Not exactly for matrimony," Rex Daviot replied with a twist of his lips.

"It is about time you settled down," Sir Terence replied. "The Daviot Baronetcy is an old one and you must have an heir sooner or later."

They were both aware that one of the reasons why

the Queen had not suggested knighting Rex Daviot was that his father as the sixth Baronet had not added anything illustrious to what had been an ancient and respected name.

At the same time, Rex Daviot was proud of his ancestry, proud of the fact that, with the exception of his father, there had been Daviots all through the history of the last three hundred years who had served their country.

"There is plenty of time," he said now.

"Is there?" Sir Terence asked. "I should have thought, considering the risks you take, that it is high time you started remembering that your son will be the eighth Baronet or perhaps the second Lord Daviot!"

"I have already told you there is no chance of him becoming that!"

"There is every chance, if you will listen to what I am trying to tell you."

"I am waiting."

"I do not know if you have ever met my brother," Sir Terence began.

Rex Daviot shook his head.

"He died a year ago. He was an adventurer and a man of extraordinary perception when it came to making money. In fact he died an amazingly rich man!"

Rex raised his eye-brows slightly; otherwise he sat quite still, listening, and wondering how this could possibly concern him.

"My brother had only one child," Sir Terence went on, "a daughter, who has been living with my wife and me for the last eighteen months. She has inherited such an enormous fortune that my wife anticipated, and so did I, that she would have been married long before now."

"What is the difficulty?" Rex Daviot asked.

He had an idea of where this conversation was leading and he also knew what his reply would be.

"When Quenella came to us after her father's death," Sir Terence continued, "she was nineteen. Because she had travelled extensively with my brother and they were continually on the move, she had never had time to enjoy the comfort and security of a home or to find herself friends with whom she had much in common."

His voice was reflective as he went on:

"She is a strange girl, extremely intelligent and well read. At the same time, I do not pretend to understand her. Perhaps it is because she has Russian blood in her veins, and we both know that the Slavs are unpredictable."

"Russian blood!"

"Her great-grandmother was Russian, a Princess who fell crazily in love with my grandfather when he was a diplomat in St. Petersburg. The Princess was a widow, but they had to wait for five years to marry each other because my grandmother was still alive—hopelessly insane—but alive!"

He paused, as if to let Rex Daviot digest what he had said, before he continued with a smile:

"Russian, English, and of course Irish blood. What do you expect of a complex, beautiful, very enigmatic young woman who as far as I am concerned is as mysterious as the Sphinx but as lovely as Cleopatra must have been at that age?"

"You paint a very glowing picture," Rex remarked with a smile behind his eyes, knowing that Sir Terence was deliberately trying to intrigue him.

"My wife entertained for Quenella, and there is no need for me to tell you that she was an outstanding success! Invitations poured into our house from all the great hostesses. The Queen herself complimented us on Quenella's beauty when she was presented at Court."

He looked across at Rex Daviot, then he said in a different tone of voice:

"Then two months ago disaster struck!"

"What happened?"

There was a note of curiosity now in his voice, which Sir Terence recognised.

"At a party at Windsor Castle, Quenella met Prince Ferdinand of Schertzenberg!"

"That swine!"

The exclamation from Rex Daviot was involuntary.

"Exactly!" Sir Terence said. "While I agree with you that he should be barred from every Drawing-Room in the land, and kicked out of every gentleman's house, he is nevertheless of importance in Europe, and he is a distant, although very distant, relative of the Queen."

"What happened?"

"He pursued Quenella in an extremely reprehensible manner. After all, he is a married man, and the days of Monarchs being expected to behave in an imperious and licentious manner are over, especially at Windsor Castle!"

"What were the young woman's feelings in the matter?"

"She loathed him!" Sir Terence said briefly. "She told me that the moment he came near her she felt repelled, as she would have been by a reptile."

Sir Terence fell silent, but there was obviously an end to the story and Rex asked:

"What happened then?"

"The Prince refused to leave Quenella alone. He bombarded her with letters, flowers, and presents, until I told him his behaviour could not continue."

Sir Terence sighed.

"It was not an easy thing to do, and the Prince was offensively rude as only the Germans can be. He even threatened that my behaviour would, if I was not careful, cause a diplomatic incident and he would have me dismissed!"

"Good God!" Rex Daviot ejaculated; then he added:

"You did not take him seriously?"

"I assure you that His Royal Highness was very serious, but I told him that if he continued to behave in such a manner I would inform the Queen of what was occurring."

"Did that quiet him down?"

"He was furiously angry, but I felt that like everyone else he was afraid of Her Majesty and would behave better in the future."

"So that put paid to the whole problem?"

"On the contrary," Sir Terence replied. "It merely drove underground what had been easier to see and perhaps easier to cope with when it was out in the open."

He knew as he spoke that Rex Daviot would understand only too well, for the sedition and the intrigues amongst the tribes incited by the Russians were always fomented by secrecy and suppression.

"What did he do?"

"He arranged, without my being aware of it," Sir Terence answered, "to be included in a house-party together with Quenella. It was unfortunately one at which neither my wife nor I had planned to accompany her. The hostess was one of our closest friends and my wife was only too happy to have the girl in her care."

Sir Terence paused, then he said:

"How was I to know that that devil would get himself invited at the last moment and take advantage of the fact that his hostess was a trusting woman and Quenella an innocent young girl?"

The fury in Sir Terence's voice was very evident before he continued:

"The Prince forced his way into Quenella's bed-room, tore at her clothes, and attempted to rape her!"

"I have never heard of anything so outrageous!" Rex exclaimed. "I have always known that he was an outsider and a bounder of the first water, but what you tell me is incredible even for a German with an inflated ego!"

"Fortunately, somebody in the next room heard Quenella's screams," Sir Terence went on, "but frankly it was a near thing, and the girl was shocked in a way which is difficult to understand."

"Did she collapse or have a nervous breakdown?"

"It might have been better if she had," Sir Terence answered. "No, she just seemed to turn inwards on herself."

He saw that Rex did not understand.

"It is difficult to put into words what happened. Quenella has always been proud. She has also been reserved and a little aloof, I thought, in her dealings with other people. I attributed it, as I said before, to her foreign ancestry, but after this episode with Prince Ferdinand . . ."

He paused, as if he was seeking for words, and because now he was undeniably curious Rex said almost insistently:

"Go on!"

"It is as if she has put a barrier between herself and the rest of the world. She is charming and attentive to my wife and myself, but otherwise she has withdrawn from all contact with human beings. I have a feeling, although she has not told me so, that she now hates men!"

"That is understandable," Rex Daviot said.

"She has refused every party and every other sort of entertainment to which she has been asked."

"Surely she is not afraid of meeting the Prince?"

"He is, I believe, still trying to get in touch with

her," Sir Terence answered, "but even when she is
certain of not meeting him, Quenella still tears up
every invitation she receives."

"I suppose she is still suffering from shock."

"I wish it was just that. I have a feeling it is something deeper, something which may affect her whole
life and her whole outlook."

He thought that Rex Daviot smiled a little scepti-
cally, and he said quickly:

"That is why I am asking your help."

"My help? What can I do?"

"You can marry Quenella and take her away from
here!"

There was a stupefied silence, then Rex Daviot
asked:

"Are you mad?"

"If you think it over, you will see that it is a rather
sane suggestion," Sir Terence replied. "Because I love
Quenella I want her to get away. I want her to be
completely free of the Prince. The only way she can
be quite certain that he will not pursue her is to have
a husband who will protect her as I quite frankly am
unable to do."

"Why?"

"Because the Prince can make an immeasurable
amount of trouble for me if I continue to oppose him."

Sir Terence spoke frankly and Rex Daviot was
aware that it was the truth.

The Head of the India Office held a post of such
responsibility that a brawl with a Ruling Prince of
Europe would not only hurt Sir Terence but perhaps
the whole system.

Rex Daviot knew that it had been a great feather in
Sir Terence's cap that he had been appointed when he
was comparatively young, but his qualifications had
made him the ideal man for the job.

That his career should be ruined now and that he

should be forced to resign would be a tragedy for Britain and, he thought, a tragedy for India.

As if he knew exactly what Rex Daviot was thinking, Sir Terence went on:

"I may be wrong, but I have the idea that even if you were willing to marry some young woman so that you could accept the post of Lieutenant-Governor, you do not know many except those of the 'Fishing Fleet'!"

This was a joke, for the girls who went out to India every year in the hopes of finding a husband were known always as the "Fishing Fleet," and those who came back unsuccessful in their quest were referred to as "Returned Empties."

Rex Daviot did not laugh, however, and Sir Terence continued:

"It seems to me a very reasonable proposition. While you need a wife with money, Quenella has to find a husband who will take her out of reach of the Prince. So, why not think it over?"

When Sir Terence had stopped speaking it seemed as if the silence was different and somehow much more poignant than it had been before.

"Are you really serious about this?" Rex Daviot asked slowly.

"I have never been more serious in my life!" Sir Terence answered. "And I will not pretend to you that I have not a lot of self-interest in your reply."

He gave a deep sigh before he said:

"I am asking for your help, Rex. Quite frankly, I am in a hell of a hole and I cannot see any other way out!"

There was no mistaking the sincerity in his voice, and it was that more than anything else which made Rex Daviot pause before he voiced the categorical refusal which trembled on his lips.

Then, as if he knew that the older man was waiting tensely for his answer, he said:

"I would naturally need time to think this over, and perhaps without committing myself in any way I could meet your niece."

He saw Sir Terence's eyes light up.

"Do you really mean that? My God, it would be a weight off my shoulders!"

"I have not said anything about accepting your extraordinary and, I am sure, quite unprecedented solution for my future and your difficulties," Rex Daviot said warningly.

"I know that," Sir Terence agreed quickly, "but at the moment I feel you are a lifeline to a drowning man."

He looked at Rex Daviot with appeal in his eyes and said:

"Perhaps you think it ridiculous that a man in my position should be afraid of a minor German Princeling, but I am afraid. I can see everything I have built up in the last year or two, the networks I have constructed with such care, the agents planted in many different parts of India who are responsible only to me, smashed and destroyed."

He paused before he added:

"Or rather, should I say, burnt to a cinder by the lust of one debauched, uncontrolled cad!"

It was obviously, Rex Daviot thought, the right word to describe the Prince.

"The difficulty is that outside these four walls," Sir Terence continued, "I have to treat him with the respect that he and his position demand."

Rex Daviot knew he was not exaggerating the situation, and yet at the same time the end could hardly justify the means as far as he was concerned.

He was also aware that the repercussions would not be particularly pleasant ones. And was he prepared to refuse the Queen's award for his services and turn down what was the greatest compliment he was likely ever to receive in his career?

It was also at the back of his mind, now that he had time to realise what it entailed, that he could carry on his work in a different way, but just as successfully, by being in a very different position in the Northwest Provinces.

No-one knew better than he did that it was impossible to bring off another coup the size of the one he had just achieved without leaving a long time to elapse.

However carefully he might have covered his tracks, however ignorant those whom he had tricked had been at the time, there would always be in the future a whisper, a gesture, a question in the eyes of those who surrounded him.

Perhaps no-one would betray the whole secret, but it might make those who were interested suspicious.

'I have to go to ground,' Rex Daviot thought to himself, 'and where better than at Government House in Lucknow?'

As he thought, he could see it clearly; and more important than the famous battle-scarred residence at Lucknow was the Governor's residence at Naini Tal among the wooded crests of the Himalayan foothills.

Like all those who worked and lived in India, driven by a spirit of service that was not to be found anywhere else in the world, Rex Daviot had developed an intuitive sense which it was difficult for those who remained at home to understand.

It was not merely clairvoyance, it was something deeper still, a sort of entering into a deeper life of the spirit which lay behind the colourful, fantastic surface of India herself.

It was at Naini Tal when he had been visiting the last Governor of the Northwest Provinces that he had stood looking up at the Himalayas with a sheer drop of hundreds of feet below him.

Above the cloud-curled summit of a snow-capped mountain-peak two golden eagles swirled and quivered against the translucent sky.

It was a picture that seemed in its sheer beauty to strike Rex Daviot in his very heart and be imprinted there for all time.

Now, unexpectedly, as he had experienced before when he had a decision to make in some crisis in his life or when he was quiveringly aware of some threatening danger, the eagles were there, omnipotent, serene, and yet strangely a part of himself.

He knew that Sir Terence was waiting. He knew that he had come to a crossroads and the direction in which he went depended on the next words he spoke.

The eagles were hovering as they waited!

He smiled and it seemed to illumine his face and sweep away the last shadow of a frown between his eyes.

"I mean it," he said aloud. "Will you ask me to dine with you?"

* * *

Sir Terence's house in St. John's Wood was a prototype of those occupied by members of the Social World who were well off but not outstandingly wealthy.

There was a butler to take Rex Daviot's coat and tall hat when he arrived, and two parlour-maids with white caps and starched aprons to assist in serving the good if not superlative dinner.

Sir Terence produced what Rex Daviot knew were his best wines, and he did justice to them, having found from bitter experience that few wines survived the heat of the Indian climate.

As he had walked into the L-shaped Drawing-Room on the first floor, where Lady O'Kerry waited to receive him, he had thought that it was stereotyped like the familiar illustrations of a book one had read over and over again.

Often when he was in India he would think of England and the cool comfortable Drawing-Rooms in which small-waisted women in décolleté gowns would be waiting, with conventional smiles on their well-bred faces, to greet their guests.

Their diamonds in their slightly old-fashioned settings would in most instances need cleaning, and there would be a faint perfume of lavender or violets as they moved.

The hands they would extend would be white and soft, the skin not dried by excessive heat, their faces not wrinkled from lack of moisture.

The flowers of the Season would be stiffly arranged in the same vases that received them week after week, month after month.

There would be daffodils in the spring, roses in the summer, dahlias, chrysanthemums, and, if the host and hostess could afford the upkeep of a country house, carnations grown in their own greenhouses.

In the summer there would be at dinner large luscious peaches and huge purple muscat grapes from the same well-ordered gardens.

Rex Daviot had accepted a glass of sherry from Sir Terence, and Lady O'Kerry had asked after the health of his father and if he was glad to be home and if it was very hot in India, when the door opened and the girl he had come to see appeared.

*   *   *

While finding his way to St. John's Wood from the Travellers' Club where he was staying, Rex Daviot had tried to imagine what Quenella O'Kerry would be like.

He had been surprised and rather amused by the lyrical and at the same time puzzled manner in which her uncle had tried to describe her.

Despite his imaginative vision when it concerned his work at the India Office, Rex Daviot had always thought that Sir Terence was a very conventional man.

There was certainly nothing unusual or particularly outstanding about Lady O'Kerry, but he had always thought when he had seen husband and wife together that it appeared to be a happy marriage and they were content with each other.

They had, Rex Daviot knew, three sons, who were all at boarding-schools, and Lady O'Kerry had once confessed to him that she had always longed to have a daughter.

"I suppose, as things are," she had added with a little laugh, "I shall have to make do with daughters-in-law, but I have a feeling it will not be quite the same as a daughter of my own."

Rex Daviot had wondered if she found Quenella as incomprehensible as her husband did, but he was sure that they would share the same feelings.

Lady O'Kerry would find that any girl who was unusual and perhaps in her mind difficult was not the type of daughter she had envisaged for herself.

He had also queried Sir Terence's description of Quenella's looks. If Lady O'Kerry was anything to go by, beautiful meant one thing to Sir Terence and something quite different to him.

Rex Daviot never worked out exactly what he might look for in a wife.

It had always seemed such a remote possibility that he should ever have one, especially with the financial strain of keeping his father in the luxury to which he was accustomed.

He knew what he did not want, and that was the type of Memsahib who was all too prevalent in India.

The difficulty there was that they had not enough to occupy themselves, having too many servants, not being allowed to make any contact with the Indians, and with their husbands often away on manoeuvres or on tour if they were civilians.

Their children were separated from them, and they were bored, frustrated women.

The only outlet was the gossip, the intrigue, and the endless parties that took place at Simla when they went there in the hot weather, or the clandestine flirtations with a brother-officer which often ended in tragedy.

A wife like that, Rex Daviot had told himself often enough, would make him want to strangle her within a few months of their marriage.

His love-affairs, and there had been quite a number, had always been conducted with what his contemporaries would have called "Grand Ladies."

India had become very social since the opening of the Suez Canal had made it so easily accessible.

Since the long four-to-five-month voyage round the Cape of Good Hope now took less than three weeks from London to Bombay, the Indian way of life had been revolutionised in many ways.

It had become quite smart to go out at the right Season to stay with the Viceroy and to make a tour of other Government Houses.

The ladies would return laden with Indian jewellery, saris, and boxes set with jewelled stones, which somehow lost their glitter and splendour once they were back at home.

The women who had found the enigmatic and mysterious young Major exceedingly attractive when he was on leave would often pursue him to India.

They wrote him excited letters on crested writing-paper, telling him of their arrival and exactly where he would be able to find them in a month's time.

Sometimes he was intrigued and amused, and sometimes he was bored—in which case it was quite easy to disappear.

The Viceroy would explain tactfully that Major Daviot was on special duties in the North and it was impossible to get in touch with him.

But by and large Rex Daviot found that such interludes in his strange, busy, and dangerous life were like finding an exotic flower by the roadside and enjoying its fragrance and its beauty for a brief period before it faded and had to be thrown away.

But although they filled a need in his life, he had never envisaged having a wife who would shine like a star at every social gathering and who, if he was not there, would glitter just as seductively for somebody else.

"What do I want?" he had often asked himself.

His ideal woman was faceless, and he told himself that he had been born a bachelor and that was how he should remain if he had any sense.

At the same time, there was not only Government House at Lucknow waiting for him, but there was a cry for help from Sir Terence, and the note of near-desperation in his voice still echoed in Rex Daviot's ears.

He was well aware that he owed a debt of gratitude to Sir Terence. All through the years he had supported, encouraged, and fought for him.

If he wanted permission to do certain things that were quite unorthodox and the risks appertaining to them appalled the authorities in India, he would always insist on them being referred to Sir Terence.

Never once had the answer come back except in the affirmative, giving him a free hand to make possible the impossible.

Marriage!

Rex Daviot had stirred restlessly in the slow hackney-carriage which carried him to St. John's Wood.

What the devil would he do with a wife hanging about, demanding his attention, his time, and inevitably, if she was rich, his gratitude?

"It is impossible! I shall have to find some other solution than this!" he told himself.

But logically he knew that there was not one except that which Sir Terence had already proposed.

Now as Quenella came into the room he found it hard for a moment to look directly at her.

He was aware that she was there, aware that she was moving towards her uncle slowly and with a grace that he could feel rather than see.

Then as he heard Sir Terence say: "Quenella, I want you to meet Major Rex Daviot!" he looked directly at her.

He saw in astonishment that she was undoubtedly one of the most beautiful women he had ever seen, and she was quite unlike anything he had expected or even imagined!

Chapter Two

As Rex Daviot stared at Quenella in amazement, she inclined her head and turned aside without a word to move to the fireplace.

It meant that she turned her back on him, and he saw that above the full flowing skirt of her evening-gown she had a tiny waist and an air of elegance which was unexpected in anyone so young.

During dinner as she sat opposite him at the table he was able to examine her more closely without seeming to do so.

He supposed it was due to her Russian blood that her eyes were dark and enigmatic.

They slanted slightly at the corners and gave her a Sphinx-like expression that was very alluring, except that her whole attitude was one of reserve and what he was sure she meant to be indifference.

He could understand what Sir Terence had meant when he said that Quenella had withdrawn into her-self.

This was obvious to Rex Daviot from the way she spoke, for although she was punctiliously polite and

courteous, he knew it was a facade and that underneath she was feeling something very different.

His work in India had made him very perceptive.

In the numerous disguises he had assumed from
time to time he had learnt not so much to think himself into a part as if he were an actor, but to penetrate
the inner consciousness of the man he represented and
actually to become him.

This had taught him to use his instinct in sizing people up and, as he expressed it himself, "finding out
what made them tick."

He found it fascinating to know that behind almost
everything Quenella said was a different thought and,
if she had allowed herself to speak then, very different words from those which passed her lips.

At the same time, he knew that however perceptive
he might be, she was an enigma which he could not
yet understand, but it would be extremely interesting to be able to do so.

They talked of commonplaces through the meal,
with Lady O'Kerry gossipping about people in Court
Circles and her many friends in India.

She was a close friend of Lady Curzon, the
Vicereine, and she asked Rex Daviot if when he returned he would carry for her a present of some books.

He promised to do everything that was asked of
him. At the same time, he could not help adding with
a glance at Sir Terence:

"It is doubtful at the moment whether I will return."

"That, I am sure," Lady O'Kerry retored, "is a
mere figure of speech. My husband has always told
me that India cannot do without you."

"Sir Terence is flattering me," Rex Daviot replied
drily, "but I admit that all my interests lie in that
strange, bewildering country, which I find more fascinating every moment I am there."

He noticed that Quenella gave him a quick glance,

as if she would like to question him, then obviously she decided against it.

The meal dragged on, and it was with a sense of relief that Rex Daviot realised the ladies were about to withdraw.

He opened the door for them and as Lady O'Kerry passed him she tapped him lightly on the arm with her fan and said:

"Now do not be too long before you join us. It is bad for Terence to drink too much port, and Quenella and I will be waiting for you in the Drawing-Room."

She did not wait for an answer but moved away, and Quenella passed Rex Daviot without looking at him.

He was, however, conscious of a fragrance to which he could not put a name.

He knew most of the favoured perfumes used often too heavily by ladies in the Social World, but this fragrance was faint, and yet he thought it still lingered on the air after he had returned to the table.

As they sat down Sir Terence looked at him.

"Well?" he queried.

There was no need for him to express more eloquently the question he asked.

"She is very beautiful," Rex Daviot said quietly.

"So beautiful," Sir Terence agreed, "that it is quite unnecessary for her to be so rich."

He sipped his port before he said:

"After our conversation this morning I went in some detail into what she possesses. It is in fact an astronomical amount, and I am told it is likely, because of the increased demand for oil, to multiply within the next few years."

He paused before he continued:

"Her fortune is also invested in numerous other commodities, the value of which is almost certain to escalate."

Rex Daviot did not answer and Sir Terence knew by the set of his jaw and the hard line of his mouth that he was hating the thought that he was to be beholden to a woman for money and most of all to one who was his wife.

He was well aware that as the law stood he would control his wife's fortune and that to all intents and purposes on marriage it would become his.

But he knew that because he was proud he would always feel humiliated that he must spend her money rather than his own.

"Forget all that," Sir Terence said, as if Rex Daviot had spoken his thoughts aloud. "Think only that you are not taking Quenella's money for yourself but for the good of India."

"Do you really mean that?" Rex Daviot asked.

"I know of no-one, and that is the truth, Rex," Sir Terence replied, "who is more important at the moment to the peace of the country which we both love."

Then there was a pause, in which Rex Daviot waited, knowing that he was to receive a confidence which was important.

"There is no need for me to tell you," Sir Terence began, "that what I have to say was divulged to me under the strictest secrecy, and I feel I have somehow to convince you of how necessary you are."

"I am listening."

"When Lord Curzon arrived in India as Viceroy in 1899, he heard rumours of Russian activity in Tibet and became alarmed."

Rex Daviot knew that Britain's position in India had often seemed threatened by Russian advances in Central Asia.

As Russia extended her sovereignty towards Afghanistan, Britain pushed the frontiers of India farther to the west and northwest.

Tibet, in the far North, once dominated by China,

was in 1900 independent and hostile to outsiders. It was a remote, cold, inhospitable land ruled by the Dalai Lama and his Buddhist monks.

"Lord Curzon believes," Sir Terence continued in a low voice, as if he felt that even in his own Dining-Room he might be overheard, "that a secret Treaty exists between Russia and China, giving the former special rights in Tibet."

"I have heard that suggested," Rex Daviot replied, "but I have always queried its validity."

"It is thought," Sir Terence went on, "that Russia has sent arms to Tibet, and Lord Curzon is afraid that there will be trouble, stimulated by Russia, on India's Tibetan border."

Rex Daviot was listening intently.

He was well aware that this might be possible. Russia had been instrumental in causing a great deal of fighting round the Khyber Pass, inflaming the tribesmen, and in consequence being responsible for the loss of many soldiers' lives.

When he left India, his reports, which had gone ahead of him in the Diplomatic Bag, had warned those in authority that more trouble was brewing and something would have to be done about it.

"What the Viceroy wishes to discuss with you," Sir Terence said, "is your original idea of having a British agent in Gyangtse."

This was a post halfway between Lhasa, the Capital of Tibet, and the Indian border near Darjeeling.

"I have always thought that that would be a good idea," Rex Daviot remarked, "but it would not be easy to convince the Tibetans of the necessity of it."

"That is why Lord Curzon is extremely anxious to see you and ask your opinion on who shall be sent to negotiate with them."

"I think I have said before," Rex Daviot said, "that

the ideal man would be Colonel Francis Younghus-band."

"I feel sure you would be able to persuade the Viceroy to agree with you," Sir Terence answered.

"But I had rather thought of suggesting myself," Rex Daviot remarked.

"I imagined that that would be at the back of your mind," Sir Terence said with a smile. "Four years ago I might have agreed with you, but you are too impor-tant to waste on what will be an isolated if important post. As you and I know, when dealing with the Ti-betans, years may pass before anything is achieved."

Rex Daviot knew that this was true, for the Tibet-ans were past-masters of prevaricating and not giving a definite answer to any request however reasonable.

"In my opinion," Sir Terence went on, "the only way anything will be achieved is by more direct ac-tion."

"You are suggesting that Younghusband should advance into Tibet and move towards Gyangtse with a military escort," Rex Daviot said quietly.

"I thought that was what you were hinting at in your last report."

"It was," Rex Daviot admitted. "At the same time, peaceful negotiations must be attempted first."

"I agree with you," Sir Terence said. "And one of your jobs, Rex, will be to convince impetuous Army Commanders that they must not infiltrate into Tibet aggressively until we are ready for them to do so."

Rex Daviot did not answer and Sir Terence brought his fist down hard on the dining-room table.

"Dammit all, Rex! Why are you hesitating? You are as bad as the Tibetans. You know as well as I do that there is no-one else in India at the moment who has your knowledge of the situation in the North."

"All right, I admit that," Rex Daviot said slowly.

"And so you should!" Sir Terence snapped. "God

knows you have risked your life often enough to get the information we needed so desperately."

He paused to say more quietly:

"How you survived that last sortie amongst the tribesmen I cannot imagine!"

Rex Daviot smiled a little cynically, but although Sir Terence waited he made no comment.

"Quite right!" the older man said approvingly after a moment. "Keep your secrets to yourself. On the Frontier, a word spoken can kill!"

The two men smiled at each other with understanding and Sir Terence rose to his feet.

"Let us join the ladies," he said, "and when my wife says good-night, I wish to speak to both you and Quenella together."

Rex Daviot looked at him in surprise, but Sir Terence, not waiting for his comments, was already half-way out of the Dining-Room and there was nothing Rex could do but follow him.

Lady O'Kerry greeted them with enthusiasm when they arrived in the Drawing-Room, and Quenella rose and went to the piano.

Rex Daviot was sure it was because she did not wish to be involved in conversation with him, and at first she played very quietly what seemed to be background music for Lady O'Kerry's gossip.

Then her fingers seemed to slide into a melody which he recognised as being of Russian origin.

It was, he thought, a song that had been sung in Russia by the Serfs, who were oppressed by their often cruel owners and who like all primitive people could only express their suffering in song.

It was a strange, haunting melody which seemed to speak of hidden things, so that one listened to it not only with the mind but with the heart.

Rex Daviot found himself wondering what Quenella felt as she played.

He recognised that her performance was good—almost professional—and he wondered whether it was just a pupil showing off what she had learnt or something which was linked with her inner self.

Lady O'Kerry, as if she had been well rehearsed, rose to her feet.

"You must forgive me, Major Daviot, if I retire early," she said. "I have had a slight headache all day. But please do not hurry away, for I know how much my husband enjoys your company. We far too infrequently have the pleasure of entertaining you."

"You are very kind," Rex Daviot murmured.

"And please come and say good-bye before you return to India," Lady O'Kerry said.

She went from the room, and Quenella, who had risen from the piano-stool, would have followed her but Sir Terence stopped her.

"I want to talk to you, Quenella."

She walked towards her uncle without comment and he indicated a place on the sofa near to the chair in which Rex Daviot was sitting.

They both waited, and Sir Terence, with his back to the fireplace, said:

"I have something to say which concerns you both and it is very important."

Quenella and Rex Daviot waited and after a moment's hesitation Sir Terence said to Rex:

"After you left the India Office this morning I received a communication which has a significance which I think you will both understand."

"Who was it from, Uncle Terence?" Quenella asked.

There was a note in her voice which told both men that she was apprehensive.

"It came from the German Ambassador," Sir Terence replied.

Watching her, Rex Daviot thought that she looked paler than she had during dinner.

Her skin had a magnolia-like quality about it that proclaimed, even as her expressive eyes did, that she was not entirely English.

Her hair was not very dark but it was not fair and there was just a suspicion of red lights in it, which shone in the glow of the gas-lamps.

It was her hair as well as her eyes which made her unlike anyone else, Rex Daviot told himself, and at the same time gave her a beauty which was unmistakable.

'A strange loveliness,' he thought.

Then unexpectedly he was aware that because of her reserve, because of what Sir Terence had referred to as a "turning in on herself," she did not attract him as such a beautiful woman might have been expected to do.

He admired her as one might admire a sculpture or a painting by a master hand, but at the moment he felt no human impulse towards her.

In fact she might easily have been made of stone for all the impact she made upon his senses.

"I received a letter from the Ambassador," Sir Terence continued, "asking if you, Quenella, would stay with him and his wife, Baroness von Mildenstadt, at their country house in Hampshire for a Ball next week."

Quenella stiffened.

"I have . . . heard about the Ball," she said quickly. "The Guest-of-Honour is to be . . . His Royal Highness Prince Ferdinand."

"The Ambassador made that very clear," Sir Terence replied. "He also intimated, in a lot of flowery but undoubtedly threatening language, that your presence was obligatory."

"Threatening?" Rex Daviot questioned sharply.

"This was implemented by the simple method of enclosing another letter in the envelope, in which he requested a formal interview with the Secretary-of-State for Foreign Affairs, the Marquis of Salisbury."

Sir Terence paused impressively before adding:

"I am to be present, and the suggested date is the day before Quenella has been asked to travel to Hampshire!"

"I will not go!" Quenella said positively.

"If you do not do so," Sir Terence replied, "if we refuse, which of course we intend to do, the Ambassador has made it clear without words that he will complain to the Marquis of my behaviour towards His Royal Highness. As you are both aware, I should then be forced to offer my resignation to the Prime Minister."

"But why? Why should he do that?" Quenella asked.

"My dear, no logical explanations are necessary when it comes to diplomacy, and the Royal word is accepted when it comes into conflict with that of a mere official."

"The whole thing is intolerable!" Rex Daviot exclaimed. "I see quite clearly how the Prince intends to bring Teutonic pressure on your niece to do what he wishes."

"I will not be his . . . mistress!" Quenella said in a low voice.

"The decision rests entirely with you, my dear," Sir Terence replied.

"But . . . can he really . . . harm you, Uncle Terence?"

"I am afraid so," Sir Terence replied. "I was, I admit, extremely frank in what I said to him when I learnt of his behaviour towards you. We were alone and there were no witnesses, but His Royal Highness will never forgive me for uttering several home-truths."

"He is lucky you did not knock him down," Rex Daviot said.

"Then there would indeed have been a scandal!" Sir Terence replied. "That of course is what I would have liked to do. But you know as well as I do that he would somehow have got his revenge."

"I should have thought that is what he is doing now," Rex Daviot said drily.

"Not exactly," Sir Terence replied. "His Royal Highness is attempting to put Quenella in the position where she is forced to listen to what he has to say. I imagine he means to apologise, then start to woo her all over again."

"I will not listen to him!" Quenella said positively.

"If you stay in Hampshire with Baroness von Mildenstadt as your Chaperon, you will have little choice."

Quenella drew in her breath.

"And you really mean that if I refuse to go, then he will take steps to destroy your career?"

"He will certainly try," Sir Terence agreed. "He may not succeed, but a great deal of harm could be done to my work which is far more important than my reputation as an individual."

"You have just told me of my importance in India," Rex Daviot interposed, "and I am not flattering you, Sir Terence, when I say that you are of vital importance to the Empire and also to Europe."

The two men looked at each other and they knew that they were both thinking how Britain felt herself threatened by the ever-growing might of the German Empire.

As if he felt he had said enough, Sir Terence said:

"I have told you both what the situation is. Now I am going to leave you to discuss it, and I would like to add that I will accept without argument anything you decide. You have your lives in front of you. Mine, though I have a few good years left, is on its last lap."

Without saying any more, Sir Terence walked across the room and left, closing the door behind him.

For a moment there was silence, then Quenella rose to her feet.

"It is intolerable! Absolutely intolerable that any man, let alone a Royal Prince, should behave in such a despicable manner!"

She stood looking down at the fire as she spoke, the flames lighting the almost classical perfection of her small, straight nose and her curved lips.

Watching her, it struck Rex Daviot that her lips were not those of a cold or indifferent woman.

There was something warm and sensual about them, and he wondered if her almost icy reserve hid a nature that was the exact opposite.

Aloud he said:

"I agree with you wholeheartedly, but I can only say that in my opinion it would be a disaster of the first magnitude for Great Britain to lose your uncle at this particular moment in time."

"Uncle Terence has told me," Quenella replied after a moment, "that the only way I can . . . extract myself and him from this . . . mess would be to . . . marry."

"Your uncle is right there," Rex Daviot agreed. "If your engagement was announced, in your case undoubtedly with the congratulations of the Queen, it would be a genuine excuse for you to refuse the Ambassador's invitation and also in certain circumstances to leave England immediately."

They both knew that he meant if she married himself, but Quenella continued to stare into the fire and again there was an uncomfortable silence.

At last she said:

"Uncle Terence said that you . . . too had a . . . problem."

"My problem is far more simple," Rex Daviot replied. "I am to be offered the position of Lieutenant-Governor of the Northwest Provinces, but I cannot afford to accept."

He felt that that sounded rather bald, and he continued:

"To be truthful I am already in debt, owing to my father's illness. My instinct is to refuse the offer and return to India as an ordinary serving soldier."

"My uncle said that it was extremely important that you should be the Lieutenant-Governor."

"It is not the only way in which I can serve my country," Rex Daviot said, "but I admit that it would make things easier for me to carry on the work I have been doing for some years. But to be frank, I have no wish to be married, and certainly not to someone I have not met until this evening."

Quenella did not reply and he went on:

"That sounds perhaps too blunt, but we must speak frankly with each other. I think it is the only thing we can do."

"Of course," Quenella said, "and may I say I too have no wish to marry anyone. I loathe men! I loathe and detest them! They are nothing but animals!"

She spoke in a manner that was all the more arresting because she did not raise her voice.

Instead, the words seemed to come from within her with a repressed violence that startled Rex Daviot, although he had expected such a reaction.

"I understand," he said. "But for you what is the alternative?"

Quenella gave a sigh.

"I do not know," she answered. "I suppose I could go into a . . . Convent. At least there the Prince could not follow me!"

"Without a genuine vocation I can imagine no life that could be more restricting, more constraining, to someone like yourself."

"Why should you say that?" she asked aggressively.

"Your uncle has told me that you are intelligent. I can see that you are sensitive and receptive. I suspect too that you have a vivid imagination."

She looked at him as if she resented that he should have concerned himself with her feelings. Then she said grudgingly:

"I suppose I must admit that you are putting into words what I have thought myself."

"I think the important thing is to think not about ourselves but about your uncle," Rex Daviot said. "The reason I came here tonight is that I am worried about him."

"He has been . . . so kind to me," Quenella said. "I like talking to him and being with him. Why did this have to happen? Why to me?"

It was a question, Rex Daviot thought with a hidden smile, which had been asked all down the centuries by men and women when confronted with personal problems.

"Why did this happen to me?"

It was the cry of those who must struggle against the inevitable even while they know they can do nothing about it.

He thought that to tell Quenella at this moment that her beauty would always be a temptation to men and that inevitably she would find it difficult to control their desires without being tactless.

It was of course unlucky that she should have incited a German Princeling to behave in a manner that was both insulting and brutal.

Now Rex Daviot said aloud:

"I think we both have to admit that we have only

two choices—either we save your uncle, or save ourselves at his expense."

As he finished speaking he felt as if he had pronounced an ultimatum that seemed to echo round the room.

Then he saw Quenella slowly raise her chin, and for the first time since they had been speaking she turned to look him full in the face.

"What do you plan to do, Major Daviot?" she enquired.

It was more of a challenge than a question, and without hesitation Rex Daviot replied:

"Because I consider your uncle's career far more important than mine, because he has dedicated his life as I have to Great Britain, I am asking you to be my wife!"

He saw her strange eyes seek his face as if he attempted to look beneath the surface, perhaps to ensure that he had no ulterior or more personal motive.

Before she could speak he went on:

"As we both know, it will be a marriage of convenience, and may I say that while I will treat you with the respect I would naturally give the woman who bears my name, I will not assert my rights as a husband nor ask any favours that you are not prepared to offer me."

They both knew that this was what Quenella had feared, and he saw a faint flush rise in her cheeks.

It made her, if possible, look more beautiful than she had appeared before. At the same time, she seemed a little more human, a little less of a stone statue.

Rex Daviot waited, then she said:

"If that is your promise . . . if you swear that our marriage will be strictly one of business . . . an expediency . . . then I am prepared to . . . marry you!"

Rex Daviot rose to his feet.

"Thank you," he said. "And now that that is de-cided, may I suggest we call in your uncle and make plans."

He did not wait for Quenella's agreement, but walked across the room and left her to seek Sir Ter-ence.

He was waiting for their decision in the small Study on the ground floor, and there was an expression on his face which told Rex Daviot as he entered that he had been apprehensive.

He rose slowly as the younger man said:

"I suggest you come back to the Drawing-Room, Sir Terence. We have many things to decide, and we need your help and advice."

Sir Terence held out his hand.

"Thank you, Rex," he said, "and though you may not believe me at this moment, my Irish clairvoyance tells me that you will never regret this day."

"I hope not," Rex Daviot answered. "I shall do my best to make Quenella happy."

He could not help a faint note of sarcasm in his voice, and by the quick glance Sir Terence gave him he was aware that the older man understood what he was feeling.

They walked in silence up the stairs to the Drawing-Room.

Sir Terence put his arm round his niece's shoulder and kissed her.

Rex Daviot noted that she did not respond towards him, only accepted the gesture in a manner that told him that she shrank even from her uncle because he was a man.

* * *

Driving back to the Travellers' Club, Rex found himself thinking that he had never after many years

of encountering strange situations been in one that was
so extraordinary.

He had never dreamt when he came back to England that such a crisis was to be waiting for him and
that within the space of twenty-four hours he would
find himself facing a decision which would affect the
whole of his life.

It seemed incredible that he should be embarking
on marriage with a woman who obviously disliked
him and who had extracted a promise from him that
she would never be anything but his wife in name
only.

But Quenella would undoubtedly grace the position
and the title to which he had now committed himself.

Because it seemed so formidable, he had a sudden
longing to be back in India.

He would much rather have been in the midst of
enemies, disguised as a Fakir, knowing that if one
slightest suspicion that he was not what he pretended
to be crossed the mind of any man watching him, his
blood would stain the ground.

He had lived with danger for so long, and it had
never crossed his mind as he entered the India Office
that he was embarking on another adventure.

Yet because it was so intimate it would, he was
sure, cause him more worry and more anxiety than
anything he had ever done before.

'What shall I do with a wife?' he wondered to himself savagely. 'And such a wife!'

He had seen the repugnance in Quenella's eyes
when her uncle talked of their marriage and thanked
them both for having such consideration for him.

"I have no need to tell you," Sir Terence said, "what
this means to me. All I can say is that I have known
you both for some time and you are both individuals,
you both have strong characters, and each in your own
way is unique!"

He gave a little laugh before he added:

"It almost seems as if the fates decreed that you should come together!"

If that was true, Rex Daviot thought bitterly, the fates had got their ingredients rather badly mixed.

He had known as he said good-night that Quenella only with the greatest effort at self-control had resisted the impulse to say she had changed her mind.

She wanted to cry out that she would not go through with what was a hollow mockery of a marriage, and, as far as she was concerned, it would be an undiluted purgatory to be the wife of any man.

Rex Daviot felt too that there was something personal about her antipathy where he was concerned.

But he tried to convince himself he was being imaginative and it was just reaction from the uncomfortable and difficult decision she had been forced to make.

There had been a great deal to talk over when Sir Terence joined them in the Drawing-Room.

"You may think I am being over-apprehensive," he said, "but I do not trust the Prince. When a man as spoilt and self-opinionated as he is is swept off his feet by love, he will let nothing stop him—and I mean nothing."

"Can you really call that . . . love?" Quenella asked scornfully.

"Call it what you like," Sir Terence replied, "but the Prince has lost his self-control where you are concerned. You have driven him mad to such an extent that he has ceased to count the cost of his actions, and that is always dangerous."

Rex Daviot knew he was not speaking without reason, and he asked:

"What are you suggesting?"

"I am suggesting that the sooner you are married and out of this country the better," Sir Terence replied. "I may sound theatrical and over-dramatic, but it is more for Quenella's sake than my own. She must be taken out of the Prince's sight."

"I agree with you," Rex Daviot said, "and as I want to return to India quickly, I suggest that you should arrange an audience with the Queen as soon as possible, then we can be married by Special License the following day."

He paused to add a little vaguely:

"I believe one has to give twenty-four-hours' notice for a Special Licence."

He thought as he spoke that it sounded ridiculously far-fetched that he should be married by Special Licence to a woman he had seen this evening for the first time.

"I will inform the Queen and everyone who will listen," Sir Terence said, "that you and Quenella have had an arrangement between you about which nothing could be done while you were still in India."

He smiled wryly before he continued:

"Now Her Majesty, with her well-known predilection for match-making, has smoothed out all the difficulties, and you will spend your honeymoon at Government House at Lucknow."

"It sounds quite plausible," Rex said.

"The person I have to convince is the Prince, through the German Ambassador," Sir Terence replied, "and I think the best way for me to do that would be to call at the Chancellery immediately you have left and give Baron von Mildenstadt the glad tidings."

Rex hesitated for a moment before he said:

"You do not think it would be wiser to wait until after we are actually married?"

Sir Terence was silent, then at last he said:

"Yes, perhaps you are right. Even at the last moment that devil might think up some excuse to persecute Quenella or even to have you bumped off! I would not put it past him!"

"Then let our marriage be a secret until we are actually on the high seas," Rex said.

He told himself as he spoke that the whole thing was absurd.

How could they possibly be so threatened by the Ruler of a small German Principality that they were forced to run away from their own country?

But he had lived too long with danger not to know that it was always foolish to underestimate one's enemies.

He also had an enormous respect for Sir Terence, and he knew that with his knowledge of men and his even greater knowledge of the motivations behind them, Sir Terence would not talk of danger unless it was very real.

"That is what you must do," he said now.

"If, of course, Quenella agrees," Rex said.

He was deliberately forcing her to express an opinion because he felt she was standing aloof from what was happening.

"I . . . agree."

Now, looking back, Rex could hear the reluctance in her voice.

It was a soft voice, he thought, soft and musical, and yet there was that hard icy quality on top of it that was unmistakable and in its own way somewhat intimidating.

Then he told himself that that was one thing he would never be—intimidated by or subservient to his wife.

She might be rich, she might be offering him as much or more than he could offer her. At the same time, in this in particular they sank or swam together, or rather they saved Sir Terence or left him to drown.

As the carriage in which he was travelling drew up

at the Travellers' Club, Rex Daviot decided he could not face his own company any longer.

He was in London, in the heart of a Capital in which there was every form of entertainment for men who were bored, depressed, or, like himself, apprehensive about the future.

The night was still young and there would be plenty of time to sleep on the voyage to India.

The coachman was waiting for him to alight but instead he shouted up:

"Go to the Empire."

Then, sitting back as the horse started up again, he planned an evening which he knew for a young Subaltern isolated in the hot plains of India would be one of uninhibited, wild, exuberant enjoyment.

* * *

When Rex Daviot had said good-night, Quenella had gone up to her bed-room.

She had the idea that her aunt would be awake, waiting to hear what had happened.

Sir Terence had not communicated to his wife the reason why he had insisted that they should dine *en famille* and Rex Daviot should be the only guest.

"But of course we must give a party for Major Daviot!" Lady O'Kerry had protested. "You know how attractive he is, and there are so many people longing to meet him."

She glanced a little mischievously at her husband as she added:

"Despite your hush-hush and cloak-and-dagger attitude where Major Daviot is concerned, I can assure you, Terence, that quite a number of people know he is in the Indian Secret Service and is the hero of many strange adventures."

"I will not have you talking like that!" Sir Terence snapped.

"I am only repeating what I have heard at tea-parties," Lady O'Kerry replied with an aggrieved tone.

"Damned women! They are worse than all the chatter that goes on in a native Bazaar!" Sir Terence roared.

His wife laughed.

"I see, dearest, that I have you on the raw, but that is still no reason why I should not give a dinner-party with some lovely women for the attractive Major Daviot."

She paused before saying:

"When he was here last year he was in love with Lady Barnstaple, but I suppose that would be over by now."

"He is dining alone with us and Quenella!" Sir Terence said. "I do not intend to discuss the matter further!"

"Why not let me ask some people in afterwards?" Lady O'Kerry persisted. "The Duchess was telling me only a month ago that she met Rex Daviot in Simla and that all the women were head-over-heels in love with him."

Lady O'Kerry gave a little sigh.

"I am not surprised. He is just the sort of dashing hero I would have fallen in love with when I was Quenella's age . . ."

She stopped, gave a startled exclamation, then said:

"So that is the reason why you want him alone! How stupid of me! I never thought of it. But of course —what could be better?"

Sir Terence did not answer, and Lady O'Kerry went on:

"I only hope that Quenella will be a little more pleasant than she has been this last week. She behaved abominably towards Lord Antrim when we met him in the Park, besides refusing every invitation that arrives. It breaks my heart, it really does!"

"Please, Betty, just do as I ask," Sir Terence said. "I want a good dinner for the four of us, and afterwards I suggest you make one of your tactful excuses to go to bed early."

"There is something up!" Lady O'Kerry cried. "I know it by the note in your voice, Terence, and I want to know what you are planning."

"I will tell you after it has happened," Sir Terence promised at last.

Although Lady O'Kerry tried to find out everything she could from Quenella, she was forced to wait patiently in her bed-room while, she told herself, things were "happening" downstairs.

Quenella, however, had no wish to break to her aunt the news of her intended marriage. In fact it was agonising to think that she must speak of it to anyone.

She went into her bed-room, and instead of ringing as was usual for her lady's-maid to help her undress, she sat down on the stool in front of the dressing-table and stared at her reflection in the mirror.

She did not, however, see her own face.

Instead she saw the expression on the Prince's face when he had burst unexpectedly into her bed-room and flung himself on her before she could even protest at his intrusion.

Even now to think of what had happened made her feel sick.

She had never known fear until that moment, fear of another human being, fear of a man who had lost his self-control, who had become nothing more than an animal.

She fought against him with all her strength, but she knew with a kind of sick horror that all she could do was ineffectual.

Then as he tore at her clothes she screamed and

screamed again, twisting her head from side to side to prevent him from covering her mouth with his hand.

That people had come to her rescue and the Prince had been dragged away from her, that she had been commiserated with and pitied, had been a humiliation almost as degrading as the Prince's behaviour.

She had felt that although everyone had expressed horror at what the Prince had done, at the same time they blamed her for encouraging him.

Only Quenella knew that he had needed no encouragement. He had, as he himself had said, fallen in love with her at first sight.

It was not a love that would have made any woman proud or conceited. It had been in fact a sheer, unbridled lust to possess her and make her his.

She had known that every word she spoke inflamed an unhealthy and brutal desire that was as frightening as if she was being stalked by a man-eating tiger.

Looking back, she realised that from the moment she had met Prince Ferdinand she should have known the danger he constituted and avoided him.

At first it had just been a dance or two at every Ball, but she had no idea when she accepted the invitation to the house-party that he would be present.

In fact he had manoeuvred the whole thing, and only when it was too late and she tried to tell him that he repelled her had she driven him to the madness of attempting to rape her.

Now, horrifyingly, in order to avoid one man she had to marry another!

"I hate him!" Quenella said to her reflection in the mirror. "I hate him, and I swear that if he breaks his promise and tries to touch me, I will kill him!"

For a moment it seemed as if there was a glint of red fire in the darkness of her eyes. Then she added:

"If I do not kill him . . . then I will . . . kill myself!"

Chapter Three

Sir Terence raised his glass.

"To your happiness!" he said. "Which I believe with all my heart you both will find."

He spoke with a sincerity which made it impossible for Quenella, who had looked sceptical at his words, not to respond.

"Thank you, Uncle Terence."

Lady O'Kerry wiped a tear from her eye.

"I only wish you could have had a proper wedding," she said. "I would have so enjoyed a ceremony at St. George's, or St. Margaret's Westminster. I had ten bridesmaids when I was married. . . ."

"And an ugly lot they were!" Sir Terence interposed.

They all laughed and Quenella knew that her uncle had avoided in his usual adroit manner a sentimental scene, which her aunt always enjoyed.

"I for one am thankful that we have been married without a great deal of fuss," Rex Daviot said.

The previous day the Queen had received him at Windsor Castle and she had congratulated him not only on his exploits in India but also on his intended marriage.

49

"I only regret," she had said in a somewhat disapproving voice, "that it is to take place in such haste."

"Your Majesty will understand that it is important for me to return to India as quickly as possible."

The thought diverted her from what he was sure would have been an uncomfortable moment if she had realised that he was to be married in a Registry Office, and she said:

"I am somewhat worried about the reports that I have received that Russian agents might have infiltrated into Tibet."

It was so like the Queen, Rex Daviot thought, to know even the most secret of secrets, which he had been sure would have been kept from her.

"We are not certain that the Russians are actually in Lhasa, Your Highness," he replied, "but the Prime Minister of Nepal, who as Your Majesty knows has always been very friendly towards Great Britain, has given us some disturbing hints."

"That is what I heard," the Queen said, "and I do not need to tell you, Lord Daviot, how disastrous it would be for the Russians to occupy Tibet as they attempted to occupy Afghanistan."

It always surprised everyone that the Queen was so well informed and also so interested in every part of her vast Empire.

But Rex Daviot knew that India was very close to her heart, and she had replaced her personal servant, the attentive Scottish ghillie John Brown, who had died, with an Indian called Munshi.

They talked for a little while longer, then Rex Daviot left Windsor Castle, knowing that his appointment and his Peerage would be in the *Gazette* the next morning.

It was therefore as Lord Daviot that he had been married to Quenella; and because Sir Terence thought it prudent, they were to leave at noon for Southampton, where they would board a ship to carry them to Bombay, from where they would travel on to Calcutta.

"You will see the Viceroy first in Calcutta," Sir Terence said, "and then go by train to Lucknow."

His voice was serious as he went on:

"You must take care of yourself, Rex. There will be a great deal of rejoicing in India that you are to join the august band of Governors. At the same time, there will be a certain amount of malice, envy, and hatred."

He paused before he added:

"But what is more important is that there will be a certain amount of fear amongst those who know how ruthless you can be."

Lord Daviot knew that he was referring to the numerous spies and agents in Russian pay whom he had unmasked and in some cases eliminated before the harm they could do could spread.

It was always easy in a country that had been conquered to find those who were rebellious and also the type who would do anything for money regardless of who offered it.

The Russians were past-masters at inflaming those who wanted a Holy War, those who wished to rid India of the British, and those who were just rebels by nature.

The Indian Secret Service was the best in the world, and what was known as "The Great Game" was served by dedicated men who gave the best years of their lives and often their actual lives to serve their country.

This morning, when he had realised that this was his wedding-day, Rex had asked himself how a wife was going to fit into the extraordinarily interesting but dangerous life he had lived hitherto.

He was determined that being married was not going to prevent him from carrying on a great many of his activities, but he would have to be very circumspect about it.

There would be no question of the Governor of the Northwest Provinces disappearing for weeks or months on end as he had done previously in disguises that had never been penetrated.

At the same time, he knew that his old friends who had assisted him in the past would want to help him now.

The strange messages that came through from all parts of India and from all sorts and conditions of men would still be conveyed to him.

It was one of the most fantastic and fascinating parts of The Great Game that no-one except a few people at the very top had any idea of one another's identity.

They were just numbers, and although occasionally they met by chance or helped one another in an emergency, only Rex and one other man knew their actual names or where to look for them.

This of course made it extremely difficult for the Russians or any other of their enemies to unravel the twisted strands which made an unbreakable rope covering a country of hundreds and thousands of diverse people kept under control by a mere handful of the British.

However apprehensive he might be about the future, Rex had to admit when he saw his bride that it would be hard to find anyone more beautiful if he searched the whole world.

Because their desire was for secrecy until the ceremony had taken place, he had driven alone in a hackney-carriage to the Registry Office in St. John's Wood, not far from Sir Terence's house.

When he arrived and saw that his papers were in order, he had only to wait for a quarter-of-an-hour before Quenella arrived with Sir Terence and Lady O'Kerry.

As she stepped into the drab, rather dark office she

seemed to light up the whole place, and Rex was aware that the Registrar and his clerk, bemused by her appearance, were staring at her almost open-mouthed.

She was not wearing the traditional white but what was obviously a travelling-gown of silken material with a small close-fitting velvet coat trimmed with sable.

Because she was not superstitious, or perhaps as an act of defiance, her gown was of deep emerald green and the hat she wore was trimmed with ostrich-feathers of the same colour.

She carried a bouquet of purple orchids which Rex had not chosen himself but had asked Sir Terence to buy for him, because he thought Quenella would like flowers that matched her ensemble.

He was slightly amused by her choice, and yet he had to admit that she looked a strange, exotic flower and one which no man would be able to ignore.

She did not look at him directly as he greeted her, and he wondered if she was shy or merely hating both him and the whole idea of becoming his wife.

There was no time for introspection, for the Registrar was waiting, and they were joined together as husband and wife by a few formal sentences and without the blessing of the Church.

They signed their names, then all together they drove back in Sir Terence's closed carriage to the house in St. John's Wood.

There, champagne and refreshments were waiting for them, and although no-one seemed very hungry, the wine, Rex thought, was extremely welcome.

After Sir Terence had managed to raise smiles and even some laughter, he said with a glance at the clock:

"I think, Quenella my dear, you should get ready to leave."

"Yes, of course, Uncle Terence," Quenella replied,

and went from the room, followed by Lady O'Kerry.

Sir Terence put down his glass.

"You will find Archerson waiting for you at the station," he said, "with the very latest reports, which arrived this morning, and a letter which I should be grateful if you would convey to the Viceroy, and another for the Commander-in-Chief."

"Anything else you wish me to do?" Rex asked.

Sir Terence smiled.

"Only carry on the good work."

"Her Majesty has been told that there was a report of Russian agents in Lhasa. Do you think that is true?"

Sir Terence shrugged his shoulders.

"It is absolutely impossible to get much information out of Tibet, but it is obvious to me that if they keep us busy on the Northwest Frontier, it might be easy for us to get slack as to what is happening on the other side of the Himalayas."

Rex sighed.

He knew the tremendous struggle it had been in the past years to keep Russia out of Afghanistan.

But beyond the towering peaks and icy passes of the Himalayas were countries, including Tibet, where the Russians could cause incredible mischief if they had the chance to do so.

He felt certain that the whispers he had heard of Russian expeditions somewhere near Tibet had not been connected, as it had been averred, with the pursuit of science or religion.

He had in fact personally been so involved with the attempts to inflame the tribesmen round the Khyber Pass that he had not until now had the time to concentrate on another Frontier.

As if he knew what thoughts were passing through Rex's mind, Sir Terence said:

"I envy you! I wish to God I were a little younger!

This seems to me to open a great many new possibilities that we have not explored before."

"I wish indeed that you could come with me," Rex replied. "But thank God we have in Lord Curzon a Viceroy who has spent a great many years in India and understands the difficulties."

"He is a strange man," Sir Terence replied, "brilliant, we both know, and yet in many ways his own worst enemy."

"I agree," Rex said. "At the same time, I believe that when history comes to be written India will always be grateful to him."

"I am sure it will," Sir Terence agreed.

It struck Rex that this was a strange conversation for him to be having a few minutes after his marriage, and as if Sir Terence had the same idea he drew out his watch and said:

"You should be leaving in a few minutes. You must not miss your train."

"No, of course not."

As Rex spoke, the door opened and they both turned, expecting to see Quenella, but instead to both men's astonishment a servant announced:

"His Royal Highness Prince Ferdinand of Schertzenberg!"

There was a perceptible pause before Sir Terence moved forward to say:

"Your Royal Highness! This is a great surprise!"

"As Baron von Mildenstadt has not received a reply to his letter inviting your niece to stay, I came to ask if there was any reason which might have delayed your acceptance."

The Prince spoke in a tone that was rude in itself.

He was a tall, handsome man of nearly thirty-five and had a Teutonic pride and arrogance that most people found unpleasant.

Although he was dressed in ordinary clothes, Rex

felt that not only his rank but a uniform enveloped him, so that it was impossible to think of him except as a soldier and a Ruler who was very conscious of his own importance.

The Prince waited for Sir Terence's reply, but the latter, obviously playing for time, said:

"May I present to Your Royal Highness Lord Daviot?"

There was a frown on the Prince's forehead, as if he resented being diverted from the subject with which he was concerned. Then as Rex gave him the bow owed to Royalty, he said:

"Daviot? I seem to know the name. Yes, of course! I have heard you spoken of in connection with India."

"That is correct, Sir."

"But I did not know you had a title."

"It is a very recent one, Sir."

"That accounts for it," the Prince said. "My memory is never at fault."

It was a statement on which obviously he had never been challenged.

He then apparently dismissed Rex from his mind and said to Sir Terence:

"Now, about this invitation. I am anxious, and so is Baroness von Mildenstadt, that your niece should grace the Ball which is to be given in my honour."

"It is with regret, Sir," Sir Terence said, "that Quenella cannot accept the Baroness's kind invitation."

"Why not?"

The question came like the report of a pistol, and there was a look in the Prince's eyes which would have made any of his countrymen quail before him.

"Quenella . . ." Sir Terence began.

Even as he spoke, the door opened and she came into the room.

She was dressed in the same gown she had worn for

her wedding, except that over it she was now wearing a heavy velvet cape lined and edged with fur.

On her head, instead of the hat trimmed with feathers she wore a small bonnet which tied with ribbons under her chin.

She looked lovely, so lovely in fact that it was understandable that the frown on the Prince's face vanished and his somewhat protruding eyes seemed to devour her.

He saw that she was astonished to see him, but with a composure which was very admirable in the circumstances she curtseyed.

"I have been trying to see you for days!" the Prince said in a voice that was intended only for her ears, "and I have called to find out why there has been no reply to Her Excellency's invitation."

As he spoke, he was towering over her in a manner which most women might have found intimidating.

But Quenella was entirely composed as she said quietly:

"I expect my uncle has told you the reason."

"No, he has not done so," the Prince replied in a disgruntled voice, "and I would rather hear it from your own lips."

As he spoke, he looked at her mouth in a manner which made Rex long to strike him.

Without hurry, holding her head high, Quenella walked towards him.

As she reached his side she said:

"I would like to introduce Your Royal Highness to my husband!"

Her voice did not tremble and only Rex's acute perception knew that underneath her control she was afraid.

"Married?"

There was no doubt that the Prince was disconcerted.

"Married?" he repeated. "How can you be married?"

"My niece and Lord Daviot were married this morning," Sir Terence explained, "and they are leaving this very moment for India. I feel sure Your Royal Highness would wish to offer them your congratulations and good wishes."

He spoke in a warning manner which it was impossible for the Prince not to understand.

Still he stood glowering almost like an animal which had been checked at the last moment when he would have sprung upon his prey.

For a long moment it seemed he just stood there. Then when Sir Terence was about to break the silence, his wife came into the room.

"I was told that Your Royal Highness had called," Lady O'Kerry said in the light, somewhat artificial voice she used on social occasions. "How very kind of you, Sir, and how delightful it is that you can wish our dear Quenella happiness in her new life."

She had curtseyed as she began speaking, standing in front of the Prince and therefore coming between his glaring eyes and Quenella's pale face.

Then as she rose from her curtsey it was impossible for him not to reply.

"Of course, Lady O'Kerry," he said, "but it is a great surprise. Why did no-one tell me?"

There was a suspicious look in his eyes, as if he felt that he had been deceived and cheated for some special reason.

"Lord Daviot arrived from India only three days ago," Sir Terence explained, "and yesterday he was obliged to visit the Queen at Windsor and receive her approval of his new appointment as Lieutenant-Governor of the Northwest Provinces."

The Prince ignored his host and again spoke directly to Quenella.

"You are really going to India?"

"At this very moment," Rex interposed before Quenella could reply. "And I am sure that Your Royal Highness will understand that we have to leave immediately if we are to catch our train."

He walked towards Lady O'Kerry, holding out his hand.

"Thank you for all your kindness," he said. "I hope it will not be long before you can persuade your husband to visit us at Lucknow."

"Of course," she replied. "There is nothing we would love more."

Quenella kissed her.

"Good-bye, dearest aunt, and thank you for everything."

To follow her husband, who was already on the landing outside the room, she had to pass the Prince.

He was looking at her and she had the feeling that he was like a man who, having received a blow when he least expected it, was furiously angry and cogitating how to obtain his revenge.

Quenella curtseyed.

"Good-bye, Your Royal Highness!"

"Then it is true?" he asked in a low voice. "Really true that you are going to India?"

Quenella did not reply, she only turned towards the door.

The Prince put out a hand as if to stop her.

"Wait!" he said.

Sir Terence moved quickly after Quenella.

"If Your Royal Highness will excuse me, I will just see my niece to the carriage," he said.

He did not wait for the Prince's reply but went from the Drawing-Room, closing the door behind him.

Already downstairs in the Hall, Rex was being helped into his overcoat by an attentive servant, and waiting, standing stiffly, almost at attention, was the Prince's Aide-de-Camp.

Nothing intimate could be said in the circumstances, and Quenella could only kiss her uncle and again her aunt before she climbed into the waiting carriage.

Rex joined her, and Sir Terence and Lady O'Kerry with a handkerchief to her eyes waved good-bye.

Rex settled himself in the corner before he said:

"That was certainly an unexpected and unpleasant surprise!"

"How dare he come uninvited and with the intention of forcing me to accept the invitation!" Quenella exclaimed.

Now that it was over, there was both anger and a distinct tremor in her voice.

"Forget him!" Rex said. "Your paths will never cross in the future; and thick-skinned though he may be, he must know when he is beaten."

Quenella gave a little shiver.

"I hope you are right, but I have a feeling that he is the type of animal who will fight to the end rather than admit he is beaten."

"A particularly unpleasant specimen," Rex said, "but I assure you it is impossible for him in his position to do anything but accept the inevitable."

"You do not think that he can . . . hurt Uncle Terence?"

"It would be difficult for him to do so now. He may try, but I doubt if he will make the attempt, since he has nothing to gain."

They drove for a little while in silence. Then Quenella said:

"I suppose really I should be grateful to you for rescuing me from such an unspeakable creature."

"I think it would be embarrassing for us both to keep eulogising over what we owe each other," Rex replied with a faint hint of amusement in his voice.

"Personally, I have always loathed being forced to say thank you ever since at the age of six I was made to write to my God-parents before I was allowed to play with the toys they gave me for Christmas."

There was just the shadow of a smile on Quenella's lips as she said:

"I suffered in much the same way, but I think it is a lesson in good manners which all children should learn."

Even as she spoke Rex was aware that the thought flashed through her mind that as far as their marriage was concerned there would be no children to be taught good manners.

He was surprised that he could read her mind so easily, and he knew he had been right in his supposition when she turned her face away to look out the window, and said too quickly for it to be a natural observation:

"I hope we will not miss our train."

"We have plenty of time," he replied, drawing out his watch and looking at it, "but I expect your uncle is rather like my mother, who always caught the train before the one on which she had intended to travel."

"It is certainly better than missing it," Quenella said.

They both lapsed into silence and Rex wondered if this was the type of desultory conversation that he would have to endure for the rest of his married life.

There would always be pit-falls, always be the danger of a faux pas, or of remarks that had a double meaning which might prove embarrassing.

He asked himself suddenly if it was worthwhile.

Was India really worth the sacrifice of his freedom?

Then he knew it was not only India which was responsible for his marriage but also the career that Sir Terence had taken so long to build up.

For a moment he forgot Quenella and thought in-

stead of a certain Pathan—code named "C-17" in The
Great Game—whose reports had saved many lives
and who would doubtless be waiting for him once he
reached Lucknow.

There was a Bengali in Calcutta, a humble little
shop-keeper in Bombay, and dozens of others spread
over the vast seething plains of India who were all
strands in the spider's-web in which the Russian flies
found themselves caught when they least expected it.

They were the people he could not let down.

They were the people he trusted and who trusted
him.

He knew that they mattered more than a few uncomfortable moments with a woman whom he did not
wish to marry and who did not wish to marry him.

*   *   *

The ship in which Lord and Lady Daviot travelled
was exactly like dozens of others which were carrying
hundreds of thousands of passengers all over the
world.

A favourite map showed a small red blob for every
British ship at sea, looking like thousands of corpuscles
flowing through the veins of the world.

Rex thought he would recognise the passengers who
filled the black-hulled *Bezwada* when they boarded
her at Southampton.

The Anglo-Indians were very easily discernible, the
brisk young cadets, fresh, pink, and assured, and the
brown, stoop-shouldered veterans, sickly from a thousand fevers.

The tired "Indian" wives with dried skins and pale
faces returning to their husbands after a brief month
or so at home in England to see their children who
were at school there.

There were of course the new recruits to the "Fishing Fleet" giggling, fair-haired, bouncing young girls, hoping that India would bring them a man who would offer them matrimony, which was the beginning and end of their ambition.

For hundreds of British families the voyage to the East was a part of life, like the beginning of term or an annual session with the dentist.

They generally met friends on board ship, and there were always, as Rex knew, endless manoeuvres to try to travel with the same crew who had looked after them so well on a previous journey.

Apart from anything else, there was a feeling of adventure when one sailed on the Far East Service in ships with high-sounding names, their high superstructures spick-and-span, look-outs alert on their flying bridges, and the Red Ensigns fluttering from the sterns.

Sir Terence had made all the arrangements and he had certainly used his influence to provide for Rex and Quenella at the last moment two of the best cabins and a Sitting-Room between them.

Rex realised as soon as they went aboard that if he was a seasoned traveller so was Quenella, and he remembered that she had travelled a great deal with her father.

She looked round their cabin, then asked the steward to bring some small necessities which had been omitted.

She chose quickly and without hesitation which pieces of luggage she required for the voyage and which should be consigned to the hold.

Then, leaving her husband to cope with everything else, she shut the door with a precision which told Rex that she was shutting out not only him but everything else which perturbed her and made her feel anxious.

Rex had thought as they travelled down to Southampton that it did not auger well that the Prince had started off his marriage to Quenella with what was to all intents and purposes a scene.

However, he thought with satisfaction that they had handled the whole situation rather well, preventing His Royal Highness from saying anything which might be explosive and leaving him in no doubt that he was now a back number in Quenella's life.

At the same time, though it seemed incredible, Rex could not help feeling sorry for the Prince.

He had known by the expression in his eyes that his whole being and all his feelings and desires were concentrated on Quenella.

She had zoomed into such a position of importance in his life that it would be hard for him to adjust himself once again to the ordinary and the commonplace.

Because Rex had studied men, because he had an understanding of them, he knew what it meant for someone like the Prince, an unimaginative German, to be knocked off his pedestal by what he called love.

To be prepared to lay aside his dignity and forget everything except that he wanted a woman was an experience which would leave a scar for many years, if not for the rest of his life.

It was difficult, even taking into consideration Quenella's beauty, to understand how she could have had this effect without making any effort whatsoever to attract the Prince.

Perhaps, Rex thought, it was her very indifference, her reserve, and perhaps too the icy coolness that he found somewhat repellent, which had driven the Prince almost to the edge of madness.

Whatever it might have been, Rex could not help hoping that this was not to be one of many incidents which would make their life together more difficult than it seemed at the moment.

They had arrived on board an hour before dinner, and five minutes before the bell rang to inform the

passengers that the meal was ready, Quenella came
from her cabin into the Sitting-Room.

By that time Rex had arranged everything more
comfortably, with the surplus luggage removed to the
hold, and books and papers unpacked and laid out
tidily.

There were flowers and fruit which had been sent
by Sir Terence and an open bottle of champagne which
was in a bucket of ice.

When Quenella came into the cabin Rex saw that
she had changed for dinner, which was unusual the
first night at sea.

She had not, however, made the mistake of wearing
full evening-dress, which would have been a social
gaffe, but wore an attractive gown of deep blue lace
with two purple orchids from her bouquet fastened to
her waist.

"I thought you might enjoy a glass of champagne,"
Rex said.

"How kind!" Quenella replied. "But only half a
glass, if you please."

He gave her what she required, then asked:

"Are you feeling better?"

She raised her eye-brows as if she was surprised at
the question.

"You could hardly be completely unperturbed," he
explained, "after both being married and enduring an
encounter with a Royal and ardent swain."

He thought for a moment that she was going to be
annoyed, but then she laughed.

"It was not quite a usual day in my life."

"Nor in mine," he replied, "so let us drink to a less
turbulent future, at least until we reach India."

When they were sitting down to dinner, having
adroitly avoided being placed at the Captain's table,
Quenella said:

"I would like, if it is possible, not only for you to

tell me about India while we are travelling there, but also I would like to read something about it."

Before he answered she added:

"I brought some books with me, but they may not contain what I want to know."

"What do you want to know?"

"I naturally want to understand the people over whom you will be ruling, and if that sounds rather a large order, may I say that everyone has to start somewhere."

"They do indeed," he said. "I am surprised that your father never took you to India."

"Papa was so busy making money in other parts of the world," Quenella replied.

She gave Rex a glance from under her long eyelashes before she added:

"It would be difficult to imagine two brothers who could be less alike than Papa and Uncle Terence."

"In what way?"

"Papa was extremely ambitious in a materialistic way, while Uncle Terence, I feel, is dedicated to an ideal."

Rex thought that this was intelligent and perceptive of her, and after a moment he said:

"That is true; and one of the things you will find about India is that there are a large number of people, both British and Indian, to whom ideals mean more than anything else."

"That is what I want to find and what I would like to learn from you. It is a big undertaking, but I feel perhaps India will mean a great deal to me personally."

"Why should you think that?"

She hesitated a moment before she said:

"I have always felt very drawn to the country, and to Buddhism, of which I know a little, and I am sure there is a secret wisdom in Asia which the West has never known."

Rex was surprised.

Of all the women he had talked to about India, none of them, as far as he could remember, had taken any interest in what had always fascinated him: the Vedas, the Sanskrit which concerned only the scholars, and the whole religious structure on which Indian life in all its varied and colourful aspects rested.

Aloud he said:

"I have some books with me which I think you will find interesting. Then, once we are in India it will be easy for you to find people to explain the different religions and the ideals behind them."

He thought even as he spoke that it was unlikely that Quenella's curiosity would survive the social whirl, the gossip, and the other trivialities with which the British women filled their lives in India.

As most of them had little or no contact with the Indians themselves, it was inevitable that they had to fill their days with more-mundane things, not the least amongst them being the changes in the climate and the inadequacies of the servants.

As if she realised that he was trying to put her off and was not convinced that her interest was genuine, Quenella plied him with questions.

They were intelligent ones and he answered them intelligently.

At the same time he was slightly sceptical, knowing from long experience that a woman would talk to him of what she thought interested him merely as a somewhat round-about way of focusing his mind on her.

Yet, if she was interested in him Quenella had a strange way of showing it.

When dinner was over she rose and led the way back to their cabins.

"Will you give me those books?" she asked.

"Of course," he replied. "I have had them unpacked and they are here in a book-case."

He found them and realised that they were only three slim volumes that he himself usually took with him on his travels.

One was of Buddhism, another a beautifully written description of Indian mythology, and the third was on Tibet.

He had included it on his voyage home because, knowing that it was a subject which would come up in his conversations with Sir Terence, he wanted to know more about the strange secretive country that lay behind the Himalayas.

It never struck him at the time that he might be closely connected with it apart from his ordinary activities in The Great Game.

Now it occurred to him that it must have been fate that had made him choose that particular volume, because the knowledge he had gained from it was something which would concern him greatly in the future.

Lucknow was not far from the border of Nepal, which lay between Tibet to the northwest and on the southwest Sikkim, through which was the way to Gyangtse, which he was to discuss with the Viceroy.

Quenella took the books from him, and Rex would have suspected, if she had been a more ordinary person, that she would be excited to have them, and yet with her he was not sure.

Her reserve encircled her like an iron fence.

"Thank you," she said coldly. "Good-night."

"Good-night, Quenella!"

He would have liked, as this was their wedding-night, to make her a little speech reassuring her that she need not be afraid of him or indeed of their future together.

It would not only have been polite, but it was what he wished to do. After all, she was very young. She bore his name, and, through no fault of her own or his, they were united in perhaps the strangest union any two people could possibly have imagined.

But she gave him no time for courtesy.

Before he could even open the door for her she had passed into her own cabin and he was alone in the Sitting-Room.

Almost absent-mindedly he poured himself a glass of champagne from the bottle which still lay in the ice-cooler, and having drunk half of it he left the cabin and went up on deck.

It was a cold night but not freezingly so because the weather was mild for early February.

He thought as he went to the rail to look out at the lights of England that were still visible as they moved down the Channel that he would have liked to stay long enough to have a day's hunting, and perhaps some shooting, before he returned to work.

In the circumstances this had been impossible, and he told himself that one blessing was that there would be no time to see his father.

He sent him a polite letter excusing himself, thinking it would be hurtful if his father learnt that he had visited England without visiting him.

"I shall be due for leave later next year," he had written in apology, *"and I hope by then I shall hear better news of your health."*

He had posted the letter yesterday and another letter had gone to the Agent of the Estate giving instructions that certain things which had long wanted doing should be put in hand.

He felt slightly guilty as he did so, knowing that it would be Quenella's money that would pay for what he ordered.

Then he told himself with good common sense that if he lived in unwarranted luxury the least he could do would be to share his good fortune with his father and with the estate which would one day be his and Quenella's home.

He was not certain how she would fit in, just as he was not certain about anything that concerned her.

He told himself with a sigh that he would try in every way he knew to make her happy and the first step in that direction would be to try to understand her.

'Girls are something,' he thought with a smile, 'about which I am lamentably ignorant.'

There were not many subjects on which he could say that, but Sir Terence had been right when he assumed that Rex Daviot knew few unmarried women and had done his best for the last five years to avoid the species.

Quenella was certainly unlike the bouncing, laughing members of the "Fishing Fleet," he had noted during their dinner in the Dining-Room.

Their high spirits, their eyes looking at every man provocatively, their obvious ignorance of the world, and in many cases their lack of education, made them as different from his wife as chalk from cheese.

Quenella, sitting opposite him, was looking, he thought, very like the orchids she wore at her waist.

Yet he was not sure if that was the right flower with which to compare her.

'More like a tiger-lily,' he thought to himself, and remembered those he had seen growing vividly gold with their black-spotted petals.

They were exotic, and yet somehow they personified the danger that could lie in sheer beauty.

'That is Quenella,' he thought to himself almost with satisfaction. 'Beauty that is dangerous enough to be inflammable for any man who attempts to possess it.'

He laughed at his own fantasy, and as he did so he heard a voice beside him cry:

"Rex! Dearest Rex! Can it really be you? I had no idea you were aboard!"

Chapter Four

"I must say being a Lord becomes you," Lady Barnstaple said with a teasing look in her blue eyes. "It will add to the glittering aura which already surrounds you."

Rex did not reply because he was used to Kitty Barnstaple's provocative remarks, with which she embellished every flirtation.

"Do you not agree with me, Lady Daviot?" she asked now of Quenella.

There was a little pause before Quenella replied seriously:

"I do not know . . . I have never thought about it."

Kitty Barnstaple laughed.

"You will find, I am afraid, that a great number of women think about Rex! As I have often told him, he attracts them as if he were a honey-pot."

"You are making me embarrassed!" Rex protested.

He rose from the chair to go to the table and refill Kitty's glass.

As he did so he thought it was a mistake for her to sound so familiar in front of Quenella, but there was nothing he could do about it.

From the moment she had found him on board Kitty had fastened on to him in the tenacious manner that he remembered all too well was characteristic of her.

They had enjoyed a fiery but brief love-affair last year in Simla.

It had not only been enjoyable but it had suited Rex at that particular moment to appear to the world to be nothing but a carefree soldier on leave from his Regiment.

Every summer the Viceroy, followed by all the social figures in India, moved to Simla, seven thousand feet up and eighty miles from a railway-line, which was one of the most extraordinary places in the world.

A small, ugly town set in a bowl of hills on the south side of a ridge, it would have been like any English watering-place except for the magnificent mountains of the Himalayas behind it.

The air seemed electrified and was thin enough to make the visitors pant at first as they climbed the stairs and sharp enough off the snows to keep them unnaturally alert and vivacious.

This inevitably resulted in Simla becoming not only a place of feverish and incessant entertainment—the Viceroy's staff numbered three hundred—but also a rendezvous for love.

Kitty Barnstaple had undoubtedly been the most attractive and quite the loveliest of the ladies staying at Viceregal Lodge.

She had made it clear from the first moment she set eyes on Rex Daviot that he was the man not only for whom she had been looking on this trip to India, but also the man of her dreams.

He was used to women falling in love with him, but Kitty was rather different in that behind her frivolous facade she had a wit and intelligence that was unusual amongst her contemporaries.

Viceregal Lodge, finished in 1888 and decorated by Maple and Company, of Tottenham Court Road, was like a shooting-box in the Tyrol, with one big chalet-like roof and two tiers of wooden verandahs.

It might, however, have been planned entirely for clandestine *affaires de coeur*.

What made it so convenient for those who wished to meet in secret was that it was too small to hold a large house-party and the Viceroy's family.

The Aides-de-Camp and many guests were therefore accommodated in various little bungalows, and as Rex was a bachelor he was given one of these to himself.

There had been something adventurous and certainly very pleasant in knowing that when he retired, Kitty in a dark cloak with a disguising chiffon veil over her fair hair would slip through the flower-filled garden, looking like a ghost to those who saw her.

She would join him in his chalet, which, built right on the edge of the hill, appeared likely at any moment to slip down into the valley below.

Their love-affair had had an enchantment about it, but Rex had known when he left Simla that it was over.

He therefore had no intention of resuscitating what had been a charming interlude while he was supposedly on his honeymoon.

The second night after she had found him aboard, Kitty had joined him on the upper deck where he had gone to take a last breath of air before he retired.

He had hoped to be alone, but she had come and stood beside him, warmly wrapped in a sable coat with a hood of the same fur framing her piquant, mischievous face.

"I have missed you, Rex," she said in a low voice. "I so often think of that small room under the stars that was to me a Heaven on earth."

He did not answer, and after a moment she said with a note in her voice with which he was very familiar:

"Oh—Rex!"

It was a cry, a plea, an invitation, but as she put her cheek against his shoulder he looked out to sea and said quietly:

"No, Kitty!"

"No?" she questioned.

"We are both intelligent enough to realise," he said, "that raking over the ashes is always a mistake."

"Only if the fire is dead."

She paused before she asked:

"Is it dead, Rex?"

Just for a moment he too asked himself the question.

He remembered the softness of Kitty's arms, the hunger of her lips, the fragrance of her hair. Then he told himself that whatever unpleasantness his marriage entailed, he would play his part as a gentleman.

There was no need to put his thoughts into words; Kitty had loved him enough to understand his different moods.

She just gave a deep sigh, then he found himself alone, the grey sea unpleasantly turbulent as they left the English Channel.

* * *

Fortunately Rex and Quenella were both good sailors, and though there were few people in the Dining-Saloon during the next few days, neither of them missed a meal, nor, surprisingly, did Kitty.

It was inevitable that in the empty Saloon she should gravitate towards them and Rex felt in fact that her chatter and her laughter relieved the tension that existed between himself and his wife.

In their private Sitting-Room now Kitty said:

"I wonder if you will like India, Lady Daviot. It is not a country about which one can ever feel indifferent. It is like a person one either hates or loves."

"I am very much looking forward to seeing it," Quenella answered.

"You will certainly find it a rival in your married life," Kitty went on.

Sitting back in an arm-chair, holding a glass of wine in her hand, she had crossed her legs to show the pointed toe of a black glacé slipper and an inordinate amount of lace under her silk gown.

There was a twinkle in her blue eyes and her fair hair was well dressed, as if she were going to a Ball.

She was very lovely and desirable, and she could stir a man's senses in a way, Rex thought, that Quenella so far as he was concerned had not managed to do.

He looked across the cabin at his wife and thought that her beauty was as cold as the snows on the Himalayas. Once again he wondered if there was any fire beneath the icy surface.

"I have never known a man who loved a country as much as your husband loves India and his work," Kitty went on, still speaking to Quenella.

"I can understand how absorbing it can be," Quenella replied.

"You will have to be very understanding to put up with the times when he works for twenty-four hours without speaking to you, or disappears in a mysterious manner!"

She laughed before she added:

"You will not know whether it is some exquisite houri who has lured him away or merely a threatened rebellion amongst a lot of scruffy natives who have nothing better to do."

"You are very knowledgeable on the subject, Kitty,"

Rex said, "but stop trying to frighten Quenella. She will have a lot of duties to perform and inevitably I shall be with her."

"Rex is attempting to reassure you," Kitty cried, "but remember my warning, and do not let him off too lightly when he produces the most plausible excuses for his absences."

Rex knew that on the whole Kitty was too good-natured to try to make serious trouble between him and Quenella.

At the same time he was aware that she was piqued by his indifference towards her and also was experiencing the usual feminine jealousy toward the woman who had married her past lover.

Kitty's husband was one of those convenient men who complacently allowed his wife to go her own way as long as it did not interfere with his own interests.

Charles Barnstaple was rich, charming, and popular. He came to India for one reason and one reason only, and that was to enjoy the sporting-facilities: tiger-shooting, pig-sticking, and polo.

Wherever sport was best he was to be found, and although he loved his wife he said quite frankly that women were a nuisance when a man wanted to concentrate on sport.

It was the fourth day out and a gale-force wind was making the ship do acrobatics when Quenella came into the Sitting-Room where Rex was working at a desk on which he had arranged his writing-materials.

He had a great deal of paper-work to get through before he reached India and he found it an unexpected relief that Quenella was quite happy to sit reading, without talking incessantly as another woman would have done.

They talked at meals, but otherwise so far they had appeared to live almost separate lives, and he thought that in this respect, if in no other, she made an admirable companion.

The voyage to India would take nearly three weeks, but Rex, who usually found the long days at sea monotonous, was beginning to think as he ploughed through the piles of documents which Sir Terence had given him that he would need every hour of those days.

He glanced up from his writing because although she had not spoken he sensed that Quenella unexpectedly had something to say to him.

She was not standing, because that would have been impossible with the roll of the ship, but had taken a chair near to his desk.

As he turned his head to look at her he found that her eyes were resting on his.

"What is it?" he asked. "Is there anything I can do for you?"

"I wanted to ask you something, if you have the time to listen to me."

Rex put down his pen.

"I apologise if I have been inattentive, and of course I have time."

Quenella glanced down at the book she held in her lap and he saw that it was the one he had given her on Indian mythology.

"Are you enjoying that?" he asked. "There are much larger and more-detailed books on the same subject, which I will get for you when we reach India. That, as you can see from its appearance, is a very favourite travelling-companion of mine."

"I find it fascinating!" Quenella replied. "And that is why I want to ask you if I can learn Urdu."

"Urdu?" Rex repeated in surprise.

Of all the women he knew in India and had known over the years, there was not one Englishwoman he could remember who could speak the language of the country in which they lived, with the exception of a few basic words with which they gave orders to their servants.

Quenella must have thought he was hesitating, and she added:

"I am very quick at picking up languages. I can already speak five quite fluently, and I would like to be able to understand what the people in your Province are saying amongst themselves."

"Of course," Rex agreed.

"I thought perhaps there might be somebody on board," Quenella went on, "who would be prepared, if we paid him, to teach me, and I understand from the Purser that there are quite a number of Indians in the Second and Third Class."

It would of course have been impossible for any Indian but a Prince to travel First Class, and even then they would undoubtedly keep very much to themselves.

"I will teach you," Rex said quietly.

"No . . . please . . . I did not mean . . . that. I know how busy you are and how much you have to do."

"I would like to teach you," he said slowly, "and it is important that you should be taught in the right way and understand how much the language varies amongst the different castes who speak it and in different parts of the country."

For the first time since he had known her he saw her eyes light up.

"If you . . . could do that," she said, "perhaps you could give me books to read, or even . . . homework to do, so that I need not to be a nuisance."

"You could never be that," Rex answered, "but we will only start the lessons on one condition."

"What is that?"

"That if you find them boring, if you decide that

after all it is too much effort, you will be frank and say so."

"Of course I will," she answered, "and you must be equally truthful if I am too stupid, in which case you can find me another teacher."

They started at once because Rex felt that Quenella was eager to get going, and he soon found that she had not been boasting when she had said that she was quick to learn languages.

He discovered, to his surprise, that she could speak Russian as well as the more commonplace European languages.

"I always hoped one day to visit the country of my great-grandmother," Quenella explained, "and as Papa was always busy when we were travelling, I found teachers for myself and directed my own education."

She gave a faint smile as she added:

"I am afraid that in consequence there are lamentable gaps in my knowledge, because I concentrated only on the subjects which interested me most."

"And what were they?" Rex asked curiously.

She hesitated before she replied and he had the feeling that she did not wish to speak of anything that concerned herself intimately. Then at last she said:

"Geography, the customs of people who live in various parts of the world, and their different religions."

"Does that really interest you?"

"Very much!"

"I am astonished!"

"Why?"

"Because they are unusual subjects for a woman."

"What you are saying," Quenella said, "is that you think such studies are too heavy and too erudite for woman's inferior intellect."

"You are putting words into my mouth," Rex protested.

"But that is what you are thinking."

A Personal Invitation from Barbara Cartland

Dear Reader,

I have formed the Barbara Cartland "Health and Happiness Club" so that I can share with you my sensational discoveries on beauty, health, love and romance, which is both physical and spiritual.

I will communicate with you through a series of newsletters throughout the year which will serve as a forum for you to tell me what you personally have felt, and you will also be able to learn the thoughts and feelings of other members who join me in my "Search for Rainbows." I will be thrilled to know you wish to participate.

In addition, the Health and Happiness Club will make available to members only, the finest quality health and beauty care products personally selected by me.

Do please join my Health and Happiness Club. Together we will find the secrets which bring rapture and ecstasy to my heroines and point the way to true happiness.

Yours,

A Personal Invitation from Barbara Cartland

Dear Reader,

I have formed the Barbara Cartland"Health and Happiness Club" so that I can share with you my sensational discoveries on beauty, health, love and romance, which is both physical and spiritual.

I will communicate with you through a series of newsletters throughout the year which will serve as a forum for you to tell me what you personally have felt, and you will also be able to learn the thoughts and feelings of other members who join me in my "Search for Rainbows." I will be thrilled to know you wish to participate.

In addition, the Health and Happiness Club will make available to members only, the finest quality health and beauty care products personally selected by me.

Do please join my Health and Happiness Club. Together we will find the secrets which bring rapture and ecstasy to my heroines and point the way to true happiness.

Yours,

FREE Membership Offer
Health
&
Happiness Club

Dear Barbara,

Please enroll me as a charter member in the Barbara Cartland "Health and Happiness Club." My membership application appears on the form below (or on a plain piece of paper).

I look forward to receiving the first in a series of your newsletters and learning about your sensational discoveries on beauty, health, love and romance.

I understand that the newsletters and membership in your club are <u>free</u>.

* * *

Kindly send your membership application to:
Health and Happiness Club, Inc.
Two Penn Plaza
New York, N. Y. 10001

NAME_____

ADDRESS_____

CITY_____

STATE_____ ZIP_____

Allow 2 weeks for delivery of the first newsletter.

"All right, I agree," he capitulated. "I think most women are charming, but their thoughts seldom have much depth. The majority of Englishwomen, as you well know, are extremely badly educated."

"Only because until recently their parents spent all their money on educating their precious sons, and their daughters were dragged up by underpaid Governesses who knew as little or less than they did."

Rex sat back in his chair.

"You surprise me!"

"Because I am prepared to champion the cause of downtrodden women? From all I have seen of the way they are treated in the various parts of the world I have visited, I think they not only need a champion but a leader to incite them to revolution."

Rex put up his hands protestingly.

"Now you not only surprise but horrify me," he said. "I have heard of militant females who are compaigning for women's rights, but I never in my wildest dreams imagined that I would marry one!"

"I have very strong opinions on the subject!"

"Then the sooner you learn to emulate the submissiveness of the Indian women the better."

"I now know what you expect of your wife."

"Not exactly."

"Perhaps the reason why you never married before," Quenella suggested, "with, according to Lady Barnstaple, every possible opportunity to do so, is that you have never found someone sufficiently pliable and submissive."

Rex's eyes were twinkling.

He was amused by Quenella's assumption of what he wanted in a wife, knowing that it was far from reality.

He had in fact, when he thought about marriage, which was seldom, decided long ago that an empty-headed woman would bore him within a few weeks.

In the days that followed he found that Quenella was absolutely insatiable in her desire not only to learn Urdu but to discover more about India.

She had asked the Purser to bring her any books that were obtainable on board ship, and a strange miscellany of lurid novels, heavy volumes of history, and badly printed leaflets appeared in their Sitting-Room.

"I wish I had known you would be interested in all this before we left England," Rex said as he threw down a pamphlet he had opened at random. "This is all the most utter rubbish and I dislike you wasting your time on it."

"All the same, it is helping me," Quenella argued. "It gives me other people's opinions and points of view. There is a book which describes the British as brutal slave-drivers, which I think will give you a new concept of the Empire in action."

"I will read it. Where did it come from?"

"From somebody in the Third Class, I think."

"If it is as bad as you say, I will have him arrested on arrival!"

He was only joking, but Quenella took him seriously.

"You must not do that! I asked particularly if I could be loaned any literature that concerned India, and it would be most unfair for us to use it against those who have been kind enough to comply with my request."

"Would it worry you if it was an Indian you got into trouble?"

"Of course it would!" she flashed, "and from all I can learn and read, the English are often very high-handed in their behaviour."

"Perhaps," Rex agreed. "But you must remember that there are only twenty thousand British in the whole of India, besides three thousand British officers in the Army, to keep order over three hundred million people—one-fifth of the human race."

"Is that really true?"

"Approximately."

"It is fantastic! Why do they not throw you out?"

"Perhaps they will one day," he answered. "That is what the Russians want, at any rate, and they are doing their best to make things as difficult for us as possible."

As he spoke he thought of the remote outposts in the Hindu Kush and the soldiers who knew day after day that tribesmen lay in ambush, Afghans brooded behind the tribesmen, and behind them all stood the Russians.

"Tell me what you are thinking," Quenella asked.

Because in a way it helped him to put his own thoughts in order, he sat down and explained to her simply but vividly the part the Russians had played in the last ten years, moving inexorably east and south, absorbing one after another the Khanates of Central Asia and preparing for the encirclement of India.

Quenella sat wide-eyed as he went on:

"They are already building a railway across Siberia to the Far East, and there is a rumor, at present unsubstantiated, of railway-building in Turkistan. This may be the first step towards planning to annexe Tibet."

As he was speaking he had almost forgotten that Quenella was listening. Now she said:

"Tibet is near to your Province, is it not? I see on the map that the southern frontier of that country is behind the Himalayas."

Rex did not answer and she went on:

"I feel that you are worried about Tibet. Am I right?"

"How do you know?"

"It is mentioned in some of these pamphlets. I also heard Uncle Terence speak of it."

"I know very little about that country, which has been for centuries under the protection of China," Rex prevaricated.

"But you think the Russians are interested?"

"They might well be."

"Perhaps that is why they have made you Lieutenant-Governor of the Northwest Provinces."

Again he thought it was perceptive of her, but aloud he said:

"Perhaps we could study together some books on Tibet. I admit it interests me, and very little is known about the whole country."

"Would it be possible for me to go there?"

"I am afraid not. In fact I doubt if any white woman has ever penetrated far over the snow-barred passes."

"It is where I would like to go," Quenella said quietly.

In the next few days she plied him with more and more questions about Tibet until he had to confess his ignorance and admit that there was little more he could tell her.

He knew that she was fascinated by the mystery of that enigmatic country and he told himself that as soon as he arrived in India he would personally learn a great deal more about it.

In the meantime, Quenella applied herself almost fanatically to her learning of Urdu, and Rex saw a light under her cabin door into the early hours of the mornings.

One night when they were passing through the Red Sea and the damp, heavy heat was particularly oppressive, he had risen from his desk to stretch himself.

Seeing a light from Quenella's cabin, he had a sudden impulse to knock on her door and speak to her.

Then for the first time in many days he remembered that she was his wife and a woman, and he needed her in a manner which had not presented a problem until now.

What would she say, he wondered, if he entered her cabin?

He could sit on her bed, talking to her, discussing anything she wished, although he was quite certain they would both be vividly aware that there were other things between them.

Then he remembered that he had given his word that he would not ask for or insist on any favours she was not prepared to give him, and that he would never assert his rights as her husband.

"Dammit all!" he said beneath his breath. "The whole situation is unnatural. We cannot continue like this for the rest of our lives!"

Yet he thought it seemed unlikely that Quenella would fall in love with him as so many other women had done.

He was aware that ever since they had married she had avoided every close contact with him, moving her hand so that it should not touch his, sitting always farther apart than was strictly necessary, and where possible preventing him from helping her on or off with her coat.

"I presume she loathes me as a man," he thought ruefully, "even as she loathed the Prince."

He could still hear her voice saying that all men were animals and he remembered the violence which lay beneath the quiet way she had spoken.

"An animal!" he repeated, and knew that he could not bear to see her flinch away from him in terror.

But that did not prevent him from going into his own cabin and shutting the door behind him with unnecessary sharpness.

The next day he felt frustrated and on edge, and

only by taking some strenuous exercise at badminton with one of the ship's officers did he feel slightly better as the day progressed.

Before they reached India, Kitty was obviously puzzled by Rex and Quenella's attitude towards each other and was astute enough to guess that something was not quite normal in their relationship.

"Why did you marry, Rex?" she asked one evening when she joined him on the top deck.

The night was brilliant with stars and the phosphorus on the water as the ship moved through a still sea was very beautiful.

It was a night for romance and in almost every shadow there stood a man and a woman either locked in each other's arms or whispering those things which should not be overheard.

"I need a wife in my new position."

"That is true," Kitty agreed. "But although Quenella is so beautiful—one of the most beautiful women I have ever seen—she does not seem quite human."

"I do not wish to discuss Quenella," Rex said repressively.

"I am not being unkind or spiteful," Kitty protested. "I am merely curious. She is not like any of your previous loves, and I have known a number of them, including of course myself."

As if she thought Rex might be annoyed, she added:

"You know I want you to be happy. You of all people need the fire of love, and I shall be very surprised if you can manage without it."

He did not answer her, and at that moment their tête-a-tête was interrupted by a middle-aged man who had been pursuing Kitty ever since they had passed through the Suez Canal.

When he went below, Rex lay awake thinking of her words.

It was true: the fire of love had always been very much a part of his relationships with the women he had known.

Like so many men who expended their energies and their minds exhaustively in situations that were dangerous, he had found relief in a physical passion which Kitty had described so aptly as the "fire of love."

He was a very ardent lover and he now faced the fact that he was going to find it very difficult to be content for the rest of his life without that passion if that was what Quenella would demand of him.

But he had always loathed the idea of being a married man who indulged in clandestine affairs.

There was perhaps some Puritan ancestry in his blood, which told him that it would be degrading and unworthy of his high principles. Yet how could he live a monk's life in a marriage that was nothing but a mockery? Or, as Quenella had called it, "a business expediency."

"We should be able to talk about this," he told himself.

But he knew he was afraid of disturbing Quenella, of upsetting her in a manner which would inevitably react upon the relationship they had already with each other.

In a strange way he felt that during the weeks they had been at sea, if she had not actually come to like him she had at least begun to trust him.

In her studies she talked to him quite naturally, as if he was not a man whom she loathed, and in the last few days she had begun to laugh and occasionally to joke about things.

"I must be patient," he told himself.

But he knew, as he lay tossing and turning hopelessly through the night, that it was not going to be easy.

* * *

In Bombay a number of officials came aboard with messages from the Viceroy, and heavily sealed Diplomatic Bags were brought into the cabin to be locked away in one of Rex's trunks until he had time to open them.

He had decided that they should go on by ship to Calcutta.

The alternative was to take the train across India, but he was eager for Quenella to have her first glimpse of India in one of the strangest and yet the most attractive of her cities.

Therefore, in Bombay they immediately transferred onto another ship and continued their voyage to the Capital of the Indian Empire.

It was on their arrival in Calcutta that Quenella for the first time was aware of her husband's importance.

As they stepped onto the Quay there were a number of resplendent officials to greet them and they were escorted to Government House in the Viceroy's carriage by a squadron of Cavalry.

To Quenella there was something very fascinating about the colourful crowds in the streets moving slowly in the hot, moist air and chattering away in many of the eight hundred languages which Rex had told her were spoken in India.

There was no doubt that she was excited by what she saw.

They drove in the open carriage with a huge umbrella held over their heads by servants wearing the Viceroy's livery of red with gold insignia.

As they travelled through the crowded streets Rex pointed out men of the Rajput States; bearded Sikhs from the Punjab, each carrying a huge sword from which he was never parted; the clever, argumentative Bengalis; and those with a Mongolian slant to their eyes, who might have come from Sikkim, Bataan, or Assam.

But what fascinated Quenella more than anything were the saris worn by the women.

They were in every colour of the rainbow and combined with wreaths of fresh flowers in their hair, which made them appear like goddesses from another planet after the dull beige crowds of London.

Government House was as impressive as Rex had told Quenella it would be.

The Palace, built by the Earl of Mornington, elder brother of the famous Duke of Wellington, was a symbol of British power.

Huge lions surmounted the gates, sphinxes couchant guarded its doors, and there were cannons on pale blue carriages.

Brilliant Indian lancers chattered through the courtyards, while thirteen Aides-de-Camp deferentially awaited instructions.

Strangely enough, the house had originally been built as an adaption of Kedleston Hall in Derbyshire, which was the ancestral home of Lord Curzon, the present Viceroy.

"It seems almost meant that he would one day inhabit it in the greatest position next to the Queen to which any Englishman can aspire," Rex had said.

"Is that true?" Quenella asked.

"The Viceroy of India has few Peers in Asia," he answered. "The Tsar of Russia and the Emperor of China are scarcely his superiors. The Shah of Persia and the King of Siam tread carefully in his presence, and the King of Burma is actually his prisoner."

Quenella laughed.

"The Viceroy certainly must feel that he is a person of significance."

"Lord Curzon would feel that anyway," Rex said with a smile. "When you meet him you will realise that he is a brilliant but unpredictable man, and he is so sure of himself that most people find him overwhelming."

They were received by Lord and Lady Curzon in a manner which was even grander than that in which Rex had been received by the Queen at Windsor Castle.

Passing through the marble Hall, with its gleaming white pillars, enormous crystal chandeliers gleaming over their heads, and bodyguards in their magnificent uniforms standing like statues on either side, Quenella had a foretaste of the pomp and ceremony in which both she and Rex would play a part in the years to come.

Lord Curzon, in fact, once the formality of their greeting was over, talked with a geniality, candour, and charm that Quenella had not expected.

However, he quickly took Rex away with him and she was left alone with Lady Curzon.

Tall and stately, she had blue eyes, masses of dark hair, and a sensitive, beautiful face.

She also had a self-possession which Quenella envied, but she was very friendly and had an irresistibly inviting smile.

Quenella found herself talking with the Vicereine more easily than she had been able to speak to anybody since her encounter with the Prince.

"You will find that you need a sense of humour in India," Lady Curzon said. "Such strange things happen. If you can laugh, they seem to sink into their proper unimportance."

"What sort of things?" Quenella asked.

The Vicereine smiled.

"One of the things I found most disconcerting when I first arrived was that if I wanted a bath, one man heated the water, another fetched my tub, a third filled it, and a fourth emptied it, each being the only person permitted to do the job, in accordance with their different castes!"

She laughed and added:

"As if that were not enough, the kitchens are at least two hundred yards away from the Dining-Rooms!"

It was Lady Curzon's American nationality which made her find so many things amusing while an Englishwoman might have been dismayed.

By the time Quenella had spent an hour or so with her, she found that despite Lady Curzon's position she was most unspoilt and had a sympathy that was inescapable.

"I must try to be like you," she said impulsively, "but I feel, Ma'am, that it will be difficult for me."

"On the contrary, I think being a Governor's wife will come naturally to you," Lady Curzon said, "and you and I are so fortunate in that we have brilliant, clever husbands on whom we can rely, but who also rely on us for the love we can give them."

She spoke with so much sincerity that Quenella felt herself flush a little uncomfortably.

How could she explain to the Vicereine, who was obviously very much in love with her husband, and he with her, that her own marriage was very different?

Then she told herself that no-one in India must suspect for one moment that she and Rex were not a normal married couple.

She had the feeling that if it was known and gossiped about that there was anything strange between her and Rex, it would not only be a tit-bit which would circulate from the Drawing-Rooms to the Bazaars but might also damage him in a way which would be extremely hurtful.

Lady Barnstaple had made it very clear that almost every woman he met succumbed to his attractions and would be only too eager to be in her position as his wife.

To be pointed at as a man who had been rebuffed by the woman who bore his name might make him a laughing-stock.

It was then, as they walked through the wide, cool corridors, that another thought came to Quenella:

If it became known that their marriage was in name only, perhaps Rex would be looked down on as a fortune-hunter, a man who had married his wife only for her money and had no other interest in her.

Quenella had mixed enough with her father's contemporaries to know what they would think of a man who behaved in such a manner, having the use of his wife's fortune while neglecting her as a woman.

Because they were men of her father's age they had often forgotten as they talked together that Quenella was present and listening to what they said.

They were nearly all rich men and money loomed large in their lives and their conversations. They were well aware that they were envied by those who were not so successful in the race for the top and that money could become obsessive and a desire which exceeded all others.

"Have you seen Crowford's wife?" she had heard one of her father's friends say once. "A fat old cow who looks like a Mexican Squaw! God knows how he can tolerate her waddling behind him!"

"He can tolerate her money all right!" Quenella's father had answered. "Worth a cool five million if she is worth a cent!"

He had laughed before adding:

"Crowford shuts his eyes when he is in bed with her and starts counting. It makes her seem quite attractive!"

There had been some rather derisive laughter at

this, and no-one had realised that Quenella was listening. But now the conversation came back to her.

For the first time since their marriage she thought not of herself but of Rex.

"Nobody shall speak like that about him," she decided.

They spent the night at Government House and the Viceroy gave a huge dinner-party at which they were the Guests-of-Honour.

There were first the National Anthem and a band played throughout the meal.

Guests were lined up to receive the Viceroy as the Sovereign's Representative, and the ladies gave him the low Royal Curtsey as they were presented.

Quenella had learnt that many innovations had been introduced even in the short time that Lord Curzon had been Viceroy.

For the first time, the house was lit by electric lights. He had also introduced electric lifts and there were electric fans in most of the rooms, while he had kept the old hand-punkahs in the marble Hall and the State Departments.

Quenella had heard him say:

"I prefer their measured sweep to the hidden anachronism of revolving blades."

When Quenella was dressed for dinner, in one of the most magnificent gowns in her trousseau, her lady's-maid brought her her jewellery-box. Looking at the many splendid jewels which she had inherited from her mother and which had been a present from her father, Quenella hesitated.

She was not certain what would be the correct thing for her to wear. She realised that there was no Aunt Emily to consult, and she knew she would hate to do the wrong thing at her first public appearance.

Quenella and Rex's bed-rooms communicated with

each other and there was also a Sitting-Room for their private use.

For a moment Quenella thought of telling her maid to ask Rex if he would meet her in the Sitting-Room.

Then she thought that that would be awkward.

Feeling a strong sensation that she did not realise was one of shyness, she walked to the communicating-door and knocked.

For a moment there was no answer, then just as she was about to knock again she heard Rex's voice call:

"Come in!"

She opened the door and saw by the surprised look on his face that he had expected a servant to be standing there.

He was fully dressed except for his evening-coat and was wearing a stiff-fronted shirt with a high collar and stiff cuffs.

There was something very attractive about the white shirt above the black satin knee-breeches and black silk stockings which covered his thin legs.

He looked almost as if he had stepped out of a picture-book of a man about to take part in a duel, and there was, Quenella thought, something dashing and rather raffish about him which she had not noticed before.

Then, because he had not spoken, she said a little incoherently:

"I . . . I want your . . . advice."

"But of course," Rex replied. "How can I help?"

"I do not . . . know what jewellery to wear tonight."

"I am sure that is not a difficult problem to solve. May I come and see what you have to choose from?"

"Y-yes . . . of course," she answered.

He followed her into her bed-room and saw a large jewel-case lying open on a chair beside the dressing-table.

The well-trained maid withdrew through another

door, leaving them alone, and for a moment Quenella was uncomfortably conscious of the big bed with its curtains of mosquito net covering it like a bridal-veil.

For a moment she felt almost a sense of panic sweep over her. She was with a man, and the last time . . .

"Now, let me see what you have."

Rex's calm voice interrupted her thoughts as he looked into the jewel-case, lifting the top tray to reveal the necklaces beneath, which matched the tiaras fashioned of the same stone.

"It is a very representative collection," he said with a twist of his lips.

Then he turned to look at her in a manner which Quenella thought with reassurance was dispassionate.

Her gown was of chiffon and lace over silk petticoats, which rustled when she walked.

When she was in Paris it had been designed especially for her by Worth, whom she had already learnt was responsible for most of the gowns worn by the Vicereine.

It was of white, which would have been expected of a bride, and it had a simplicity and at the same time a *chic* which Rex, with his experience of women, recognised and appreciated.

"Diamonds tonight, I think," he said at length. "They will expect you to look young and bridal and at the same time to glitter."

He smiled as he added:

"You can certainly do that, and you might as well give everybody a treat while you are about it."

"Is that what it will be?" Quenella asked.

"You will also cause a great deal of envy, hatred, and malice in a lot of female breasts, and why not?"

Quenella was listening, and he added:

"If you dress down, they will say you are dull or think it an insult. If you look like the Fairy Queen on top of the Christmas-tree, they can merely grit their teeth and wish they could annihilate you."

Quenella laughed unaffectedly.

"You make it sound like a game!"

"Have you not learnt already that that is what it is —a game of one-upmanship? Tonight you are Number Two on the spiral staircase. When we reach Lucknow you will be Number One."

"You are making me nervous," she said accusingly.

"Put on that diamond bauble," he said, "hang the necklace round your neck, and tell them to keep their criticism to themselves. It never matters what people think, it is what they say to your face that is disconcerting."

"Is that your creed?" Quenella flashed.

"I never give my enemies the satisfaction of thinking of them," he replied.

He took the diamond tiara which had belonged to Quenella's mother out of the jewel-case.

"Shall I help you to put it on?"

"My maid will do it," Quenella replied quickly.

"Of course," Rex agreed. "I will wait in the Sitting-Room until you are ready."

He moved away through the communicating-door, and Quenella stood for a moment with the tiara in her hands, watching him go.

"I might have let him help me," she thought to herself.

Then she waited for the shudder that such an idea would normally evoke in her.

To her surprise, it did not come!

Chapter Five

"This is very exciting!" Quenella said.

"Do you mean the train?" asked Rex, who was sitting opposite her.

"No, I mean being able to see the countryside. That is what I have been looking forward to."

They were travelling northwest to Lucknow, and the Viceroy with unusual generosity had provided them with two coaches from his special train.

Rex knew that it had been built for the Prince of Wales's visit in 1875 and by now it was beginning to fall apart.

It consisted of twelve cream and gold coaches hauled by two steam-engines, and when the Viceroy used it to move about the country, civilian and military Secretaries, two Doctors, and some hundred other members of the staff were housed on board.

A pilot engine ran ahead, and the whole length of the line was guarded by levies from each village in its vicinity.

It was a great tribute to Rex Daviot's importance and his new position that two of the splendid coaches had been attached to the ordinary train that carried a massive number of passengers.

Rex was used to the hurly-burly of Indian railway-stations, but to Quenella the crowd at Howrah was a fascinating new experience.

There were families camping on the platforms, sleeping, cooking, and eating, until it was their turn to become part of the crowds packed cheek-by-jowl into the Third Class carriages.

There was a bedlam of noise from water-vendors, newspaper-boys, peddlars of rice and sweet-meats, and tea-serving waiters, all jostling and yelling, their voices joining with the noise of the screaming children, shouting porters, and whistling locomotives.

It was in fact complete pandemonium.

"Even so," Rex remarked, "the trains run on time."

All hours of the twenty-four are alike to Easterners and their passenger traffic was regulated accordingly.

They had been seen off by a great number of officials and of course the Viceroy's private servants in their red and gold uniforms.

As they walked towards their sentry-guarded coaches they heard long and furious arguments taking place between the Indian travellers and the Eurasian ticket-collectors.

Rex explained to Quenella that the natives thought that the tickets they bought were magic pieces of paper and were furious that strangers should punch great pieces out of their charms.

It certainly amused Quenella when the guard approached to ask if he could have Rex's permission to start the train. As he gave it solemnly, he saw that her eyes were twinkling with amusement.

"Does that always happen?" she asked.

"Always when the train carries an important Englishman," he replied.

They both laughed.

"I cannot imagine such a thing occurring in England or in any other part of the Western World."

"In India the British are the conquering race and are treated with just respect," Rex replied.

But she knew he was mocking himself.

With a great deal of whistling steam from the engine sounding over everything else, they started off, and once they were away from Calcutta, looking out the window Quenella could see the varying aspects of the country as she wished to do.

When they first left the city the landscape was flat and much of it was waterlogged, but now Quenella could see the white bullocks at work in the fields, and water-buffaloes standing in the water-tanks which were outside every village.

She had occasional glimpses of a camel silhouetted against a cloudless sky.

"It is what I thought India would be like," she said after a little while, almost as if she spoke to herself.

"Why?" Rex asked.

She hesitated and he thought that she was choosing her words. Then she said, almost as if she could not help telling the truth:

"It is like coming . . . home."

He looked surprised, then he asked:

"Why do you say that?"

"Because that is what it . . . feels like to . . . me. I have always wanted to come . . . East, I have known too that it was India which . . . drew me."

She thought he looked incredulous, then she said:

"When I read the books you gave me it was as if I had read them . . . before, and everything they told me was . . . already there . . . inside myself."

She made a little gesture with her hands, then she said:

"Perhaps you do not understand, and it is difficult to put into words."

"But I do understand," he said. "It is what I also feel, what I have always felt, that I belong."

She looked at him and he knew that her eyes searched his face as if she could hardly believe what she had heard.

Then she turned once again to look out at the passing countryside.

Later in the evening she went to her own sleeping-compartment to rest.

"Have we been given coaches used by the Viceroy personally?" she had asked Rex.

"No," he had replied. "His consists of a bed-room, a bath, and a Saloon, comprising one carriage, and the Vicereine has another to herself. Ours is used by the most important guests travelling with them."

The compartments were obviously smaller, and they were sharing a coach, but it was most comfortably furnished, and Quenella had learnt from her maid that hot water for her bath would be taken out at prearranged points where it had been heated in huge vats.

This was something to look forward to because it was very hot, and Quenella undressed to lie on her comfortable bed thinking not of herself but of India.

She felt a strange excitement creeping over her at the thought of reaching Lucknow.

How could she have known or even imagined a month ago that she would be married and find herself in what she now knew was a very important position in a country that brought her sensations she had never felt before?

Undoubtedly they were there, and she found herself thinking of the diverse people, each with their own caste and religion, each part of the great crowded country which even without the British was a power in itself.

The frontier ran from the Bay of Bengal to the Pamirs and on to Karachi, and the sea coast was about three thousand miles long. One-tenth of the entire trade of the British Empire passed through the ports of India.

It was fascinating, she thought, like one of the patchwork quilts she had seen old ladies making in English and American villages, where tiny pieces of hundreds of different materials in brilliant colours made up an intricate pattern.

After her bath, which she enjoyed and tried not to think of the immense amount of labour it had involved, she put on one of the elegant, loose-fitting tea-gowns which had just come into vogue among the fashionable ladies in London.

It had been invented for the hours of rest that were taken from tea-time to the hour when they changed into something far more elaborate for dinner.

It was always worn by those who entertained the Prince of Wales. To do so, the lady who was to be honoured by his presence lay on a cushion-covered couch, with the curtains drawn and the room sprayed with expensive perfume.

There was a great deal of gossip about these tea-parties at which the heir to the throne was the only guest and the hostess was beautiful and alluring enough to catch his ever-roving eye.

But despite the manner in which those who were not so privileged looked down their noses, the tea-gown was such a convenient garment that it had come to stay.

Besides, what woman could resist removing her tightly laced corset and being able to breathe freely for at least two hours?

The tea-gown that Quenella wore was a very attractive one, of pale lilac chiffon which swirled in frills round her feet and with which she wore a long necklace of pale amethysts set with diamonds.

When she came into the Sitting-Room and Rex rose

to his feet he thought he had never seen her look more beautiful, and there was too, he noticed, a different expression on her face from the one to which he had become accustomed.

He hardly liked to admit it to himself, but he was certain that some of her reserve and icy coolness had gone and that there was a new eagerness about her which he had not noticed before.

"There is so much I want to ask you," she said.

She sat down in an arm-chair at the table on which they were to dine, and opening a book she started at once on a long questionnaire about Vishnu, the Preserver of the Universe.

Rex began by quoting from Vishnu:

> *"I am the self in the inmost heart of all that*
> *are born*
> *I am the beginning, the middle, the end of all*
> *creation ..."*

"I am trying to understand that," Quenella murmured.

"Vishnu's most important incarnation was as Krishna," Rex said.

Quenella did not speak and he went on:

"Krishna is of course the Hindu expression of personal human love. Girls think of him as the ideal man and lover, and he has inspired much of India's art."

As he spoke he wondered if Quenella, having, he was quite certain, no desire to speak of love, would quickly change the subject, but instead she said reflectively:

"Krishna is the dancing god and is usually depicted playing a pipe."

"That is right," Rex agreed.

"Your book tells how avidly he is worshipped."

"I think everyone, whoever he may be, seeks love."

There was a little silence, then Quenella said:

"Krishna surely exemplifies perfect love. Does anyone ever find that?"

"I think it is what all human beings seek, the ideal that they hold in their hearts."

"Is that what . . . you want?" Quenella asked.

He knew it was an effort for her to formulate the question, and he deliberately replied in an impersonal tone of voice:

"Of course. I am no different from anyone else. I have always sought the love that is expressed so clearly in the Sanskrit writings, and I have hoped that Krishna would eventually bring me the woman of my dreams."

He felt that what he had said disturbed her, and Quenella was silent for some moments before she said:

"I have . . . dreamt too."

"You would not be human," Rex agreed, "if you had not thought one day the fairy-stories would come true and you would find Prince Charming and live happily ever afterwards."

"That is . . . only a story."

"But it happens."

"And now we know it cannot . . . happen to . . . us."

Before he could answer she added:

"It may happen to . . . you. After all, Lady Barnstaple said . . ."

"I think you are aware," Rex interrupted, "that we are talking of a very different type of love from what Lady Barnstaple chatted about and which is the common currency of the gossip-mongers."

"You are quite certain that it is different?"

"Absolutely certain!" Rex replied. "The flirtations and the heart-aches that are part of a man's and a woman's growing up are only a shadow of the real thing."

She looked at him with startled eyes and he went on:

"It is like the foothills of the Himalayas, which as you will see are very beautiful, but when one is there one is always deeply conscious that above, out of reach, are the peerless peaks, the untrod snows which challenge every man who sees them."

"I understand what you are saying," Quenella murmured, "but no-one yet has reached the summit of the highest mountain of the Himalayas."

"I used it just as a simile; but the more you read, the more you study human beings, you will find that some do attain the unattainable."

He knew by the expression on her face that that was what she wished to do. As he watched her across the table he thought that most of the women he had known had been very content in the foothills and had no wish to go higher.

As soon as dinner was finished Quenella arose, saying:

"It has been a long day and we were late last night. I think we would both be wise to retire early."

"I have some work to do," Rex replied, "but I hope that you will sleep well."

"I usually do on a train," Quenella replied. "The movement and the mumble of the wheels rock me to sleep."

"Then good-night, Quenella. I hope what we see tomorrow will interest you."

"I am sure it will," she replied.

She moved with perfect balance through the door which led into her sleeping compartment.

Rex watched her go; then, although he opened a despatch-case which was standing by his side, he found it difficult to settle at once to the papers which required his attention.

She was certainly different, he told himself, different from the withdrawn, icily cold woman he had mar-

ried, who he knew had been tense with fear or hatred
every time he came near her.

Tonight Quenella had talked to him in a relaxed
manner, and he had the feeling, although he could not
be sure, that when they had spoken of love her
thoughts had not immediately turned to the Prince.

Perhaps she was forgetting, perhaps the horror the
brute had aroused in her was receding.

If anything could effect the miracle of forgetfulness,
Rex was certain it was India.

It was strange, he told himself, that Quenella should
feel she "belonged."

If any other woman had said such a thing he would
have suspected that she did so intentionally to focus
his attention on herself, or, more insidiously, just to
please him.

Quenella had spoken in a manner which told him
that it was the truth which came from her lips.

Unlike Kitty and the other women he had known
intimately, she had never made the slightest effort to
attract him or hold his interest.

"Whatever her feelings for me," he said to himself,
"I find her a strange and interesting phenomenon, not
so much as a woman but rather as a human being."

* * *

In her own compartment Quenella allowed her maid
to undress her and put on a very fine muslin nightgown
inset with lace.

Light though the material was, it still was restricting
in the heavy heat, which made the cabin seem stifling
despite an electric fan.

Quenella thought with commiseration of the passengers in the Third Class compartments, who, packed

like sardines, would find it hard to breathe, let alone to sleep.

"One is never grateful enough," she remembered her father saying once, "for the small comforts of life."

She thought as she lay down on her bed, her back against the soft pillows, that this was in fact quite a big comfort.

She turned on her reading-lamp and picked up her books.

There was so much more, she thought, that she wanted to ask Rex, but she had no wish to bore him and he had been so exceptionally kind in teaching her Urdu all the time they had been sailing to India.

She supposed now her lessons would end, and she thought that however many other teachers she might employ, they would none of them have the same capacity for making everything they discussed so interesting.

Rex also gave her in every lesson something personal and intimate to take away.

At night she would go over and over again everything they had discussed, and she knew that because he had been her teacher and had told her what she longed to know, she had ceased to be afraid of him as a man.

'Papa would think I was very lucky to have married him,' she thought to herself.

Just for a moment the terror the Prince had evoked was there, his evil face staring at her from the shadows of the compartment.

Then it seemed as if Krishna, the God of Love, was with her.

She could see his slim figure, the exquisite grace of his hands playing on his pipe, a smile on his lips.

Krishna, God of Love!

Almost without her consciously willing it, as the vision appeared in her mind she prayed:

"Give me love, Krishna. Lord Krishna, give me love!"

* * *

Quenella must have slept until she awoke as the train rumbled into a station and there was the usual hubbub on the platform, which by now she had heard half-a-dozen times.

Her maid had pulled down the dark blinds, and Quenella knew that the moment the train stopped, the soldiers who accompanied them as guards would stand in front of Rex's carriage and hers.

The screaming voices seemed to increase and she thought there were several men shouting louder than the rest.

She would have liked to look out, but, knowing it was indiscreet to raise the dark blinds, she rose from her bed to go to the other side of the carriage.

It was impossible while they were travelling to have the window open, because of the dust which would blow in like a heavy film and settle on everything.

But it was worthwhile even for a few moments, Quenella thought, to breathe air which was not being churned round and round by an electric fan.

She pulled up the Venetian blinds and opened first the gauze curtain and then the glass window. Across the railway-tracks she could see another platform, but there was no commotion on it, only piles of luggage and a number of dark bodies rolled up like carpets, which she knew were men asleep.

She raised her eyes and saw the stars brilliant in the sky above.

The air was heavy, and although she breathed deeply she still felt almost suffocated by the heat.

Then suddenly she heard a whisper from below her and someone said in English:

"Open the door! For God's sake, open the door!"

She peered down, but it was impossible to see anything in the darkness.

She thought she must have been mistaken in what she had heard. But then it came again:

"Open the door, I beg of you! Quickly! There's no time!"

Because the plea was in English, Quenella did not stop to think but did as she was told, lifting the throw-over catch which was fitted to all Indian carriages.

Even as she did so someone pushed past her into the compartment.

The reading-lamp by the bed was the only light and it was covered by a heavy green shade, so for the moment it was difficult to see who had entered.

But she knew that it was a man.

He closed the door and pulled down the blinds so quickly it was almost in one movement.

Then as he turned towards Quenella she stared at him in horror.

She saw that he was dark-skinned and there was a cut on his face which was pouring with blood.

His clothes, which were exceedingly dirty, were torn and blood-stained.

As he looked at her she tried to scream, but she was too shocked and horrified at the moment for any sound to come from between her lips.

Suddenly he staggered, doubled up in a strange manner, and collapsed in a heap at her feet.

Then she knew she must scream, but before she could do so he muttered:

"Daviot—fetch . . . Daviot!"

The mere fact that he was still speaking English despite his appearance prevented Quenella from calling for the guard on the platform outside the carriage.

Instead she looked down at the man sprawled on the floor and saw that blood apparently coming from his side was staining the carpet.

His eyes were closed, but his lips moved and once again he said:

"Daviot!"

Trembling so violently that it was hard to open the door into the Sitting-Room, Quenella managed it and found that the room was in darkness.

Guided by the light that came from between the blinds which covered the windows, she moved on her bare feet towards the door which led to Rex's compartment.

Because she was so frightened and bemused she did not knock.

A reading-light illuminated the bed but she saw that he was lying asleep, a number of papers beside him.

He was naked to the waist and she knew that like herself he had been trying to avoid the oppressive heat.

She had no time to think of anything, not even the fact that she was seeing her husband unclothed for the first time.

"Rex!"

Her voice was strangled in her throat and it was obvious that he had not heard her.

Without thinking what she should do, she put her hand on his arm.

"Rex!" she said again.

He was in the heavy sleep of a man who is exhausted, but his eyes opened and instantly he was awake with that alertness which comes to those who are constantly in danger.

For a moment he stared at her incredulously. Then he exclaimed:

"Quenella!"

"There is . . . there is a . . . man in my . . . compartment."

"A man?"

Rex sat up abruptly and Quenella felt that he might be about to call one of the soldiers posted outside.

"He asked for you . . . by name," she said. "He is wounded . . . bleeding."

Without a word Rex sprang off the bed, and, tightening the loin-cloth he wore round his waist, he entered the Sitting-Room and Quenella followed him into her own compartment.

The man was lying where she had left him and she thought that he must be dead, for even allowing for the darkness of his skin, his face seemed bloodless and his lips were almost white.

Rex knelt down beside him.

"Who are you?" he asked gently.

"E-Seventeen—Sir. They—almost got—me!"

The words came with difficulty from between his lips.

Supporting the man with one arm under his head, Rex looked round at Quenella.

"There is a first-aid box on the table by my bed."

Quenella ran back to fetch it, and when she returned she saw that Rex had put a pillow under the man's head and had pulled off the dirty garments he wore above the waist.

Quenella now saw that he was bleeding from a knife-wound in his side, and the blood from the cut on his cheek was also running onto his chest.

"Water!" Rex said. "But first open the box for me."

Quenella did as she was told, then fetched from the bath-room some water in a small basin and a sponge.

"Towels! As many as you can find!" Rex commanded. "There are some more in my compartment."

When she returned with the towels the man's eyes were open and she saw Rex give him something to swallow.

He began to murmur:

"I'm—sorry, Sir. They—were on to me—yesterday —I—escaped and—travelled here in—a bullock-cart —but there were—three of them at the—station."

It was obviously very difficult for him to speak, and yet whatever Rex had given him was beginning to make it easier and he went on:

"There is—information I have to—get to B-Twenty-nine in—Delshi."

"I will see that he gets it. Where is it hidden?"

"In my—hair."

Rex undid the dirty turban, and the man's hair, not very long but so black that it might have been dyed, tumbled round his blood-stained cheeks.

Quenella saw Rex take a small piece of paper from it and place it in the cloth that encircled his waist. Then he said:

"You will have to get off the train. They will suspect you might be on it."

"I don't—matter—Sir—now that you—have the —information."

"Of course you matter," Rex said. "We cannot afford to lose anyone in The Great Game."

"No, Sir—but you must—not be involved—with me."

"I do not intend to be!"

Quenella stared at Rex in horror.

Surely he was not going to leave this man bleeding and utterly exhausted when there were enemies outside who were obviously intent upon destroying him?

Then she saw her husband smile.

"I had better change your appearance a little. Do you feel like sitting up?"

The man gave a weak smile.

"I am—much better. How much—opium did you —give me?"

"Enough to take away the pain," Rex replied. "When did you last eat?"

"Two—it might have—been three—days ago. It's hard to—remember."

Rex looked up at Quenella.

"We cannot ask for anything," he said, "but there might be something on the side-table."

"I will go and look," Quenella said.

She went into the Sitting-Room, switched on one of the small lamps, and began to search.

There was a table on which the waiters had placed food when they had served their dinner. Now it was empty except for a white cloth.

Then she saw that with the rocking of the train, one of the thick slices of bread which had been served at dinner was lying on the floor.

She picked it up.

It might not be very hygienic to eat it, she thought, but at least it was better than starving.

She took it to Rex and saw that he was skillfully, in a way that told her he was an expert, bandaging the wound in the man's side.

"You must get to a Doctor and have this stitched as soon as possible," he said.

"There is a—Doctor who will—help me if I can—reach the next town."

"You will manage that," Rex said confidently.

"This was all I could find," Quenella said, holding out the piece of bread.

The man on the floor took it from her and devoured it hungrily like a dog who has not eaten for a long time.

"I have remembered there is some chocolate in my dressing-case," Rex said, "and will you at the same time bring my razors?"

She looked at him in surprise, but again she obeyed without question.

She found the razors in a neat leather case and the chocolate was in a packet such as was issued to soldiers when they are on manoeuvres.

She took it back to her compartment and as she entered she saw to her astonishment that Rex was cutting the man's hair with a pair of scissors that had been in the first-aid box.

The small pieces fell to the floor round him.

"You are going to be a Buddhist monk," Rex said. "No-one will touch a Holy Man, and there is a cover on my bed which is almost the right colour."

This time Quenella did not wait for the order for her to fetch it, but went back into Rex's bed-room. She found the bed-spread, which was an attractive golden yellow, and laid it down on her own bed.

The man was now devouring the chocolate almost as quickly as he had wolfed down the bread.

Rex was shaving his head, making him as bald as the Buddhist monks she had seen in their golden robes moving through the crowds in the streets of Calcutta.

"That is a good dye you are using," Rex said as he worked.

"It's the one—recommended," E-Seventeen replied, "but I put it on rather—thicker than—usual. It is going to be a devil of a job—to remove it."

"When are you due back?" Rex enquired.

"In another two weeks. The C.O. is very understanding. I do not know who spotted me—but how do we ever know?"

"How indeed!" Rex agreed.

He had finished shaving the man's head and he looked very different from the man who had entered Quenella's compartment.

Some salve which Rex had applied to his face had stopped the bleeding, and the opium had dilated his eyes, giving him an entirely different expression.

"See if you can stand on your feet," Rex suggested.

Without being told, but knowing it was expected of her, Quenella withdrew to the Sitting-Room.

A few minutes later Rex came in to pass through to his bed-room.

"We have another four minutes before he must leave here," he said. "It would be a mistake to run it too fine."

She longed to ask him half-a-dozen questions, but she knew that he was too busy to listen.

He came back from his own bed-room with money in his hand, and now because she was curious she followed him into her compartment.

The man she had saved was standing on his feet and certainly it would have been hard to recognise him.

The yellow bed-spread was draped over his shoulder. Above it, his head, shaved of every hair, gave him the benign, aesthetic appearance of the priestly followers of Buddha.

Rex gave him the money and several tablets which Quenella knew were opium.

"Use them sparingly," he said, "but they will keep you going until you reach safety."

He looked round the compartment and saw on the dressing-table a small silver bowl which contained pot-pourri. He emptied it and held it out to E-Seventeen.

"Your begging-bowl!"

The man smiled.

"I knew that if I could reach you, Sir, you'd save me."

" 'Never assume the journey is over until one has reached home,' " Rex replied, quoting an Indian proverb.

E-Seventeen looked at Quenella.

"Thank you, Ma'am. I hope I didn't frighten you, but when you looked out that window I knew it was my only chance."

"I am so glad I could help," Quenella replied.

They were the first words she had spoken since she had awakened Rex.

"You had better go!" Rex said.

He raised the blind and latched the door through which E-Seventeen had entered the compartment.

Then he leant out casually, as if he was taking the air.

After staring up at the sky for a moment, he looked to the right and the left, then opened the door.

"God bless you!" E-Seventeen said as he passed Quenella.

He let himself down very carefully onto the railway-track, as if he was afraid of starting his wound bleeding, then he moved in the darkness across the lines to climb up onto the opposite platform.

For a moment he seemed to hesitate, then as they watched him he lowered himself down beside two or three of the other sleepers.

"That was intelligent of him," Rex whispered.

"But why does he not get away at once?" Quenella asked.

Rex shut the window and pulled down the blind.

"Because," he replied, "those who are searching for him are watching the exits and for the next few hours will scrutinise anybody who leaves the station."

"Of course! I understand!" Quenella exclaimed.

She looked up at Rex standing beside her and asked:

"What will you do with the message he gave you? How will you get it to the man in Delhi?"

"What message—and what man?" Rex asked.

He spoke teasingly, but she understood that he was telling her without words to forget everything that had happened.

He started to pick up the black hair from the floor, the dirty clothes that E-Seventeen had worn, and some blood-stained pieces of cotton-wool he had used, and rolled them all up together.

Then he looked ruefully at the stains of blood on the pale carpet.

"I will remove those," Quenella said.

"How?" he asked.

"With cold water," she answered.

"Yes, of course," he said. "But I will do it for you."

He took one of the towels and scrubbed vigorously. The blood-stains disappeared, but the towel looked even worse than it had before.

As if Quenella had asked him the question, he said:

"Do not worry. When we are a long way farther north I will dispose of the towels as well as the other things."

He looked round as if to see if there was any further evidence left of their visitor.

"I wish we could have given him something more substantial to eat," Quenella said.

"He will manage now that he has money," Rex answered.

"Opium takes away hunger; besides, one can always obtain merit by feeding a Holy Man."

"It was very clever of you to disguise him, and I cannot believe that anyone, even his own mother, would recognise him. Is he English?"

"Who are we talking about?" Rex enquired.

Quenella gave a little sigh.

"You are being very unkind. I did let him in, and I did not scream."

"You behaved admirably," Rex said in a different tone of voice, "and it was exactly what I would have expected of you."

"Are you saying that to please me, or because I really did well?"

Quenella was like a child asking for his approval.

"You have done very well," he said, "and because you are my wife, this sort of thing might happen again. Tomorrow when we have time I will tell you one or two of the things you are bursting with curiosity to know."

"I admit that is true," Quenella said with a smile.

Her eyes met his and for the first time she was conscious that she was wearing nothing but a transparent nightgown and that he was naked to the waist.

She had been so intent on what was happening and wanted so desperately to save the man who had been wounded that she had been completely unaware of herself or of her husband as a man.

Now as the colour rose in her cheeks he said quickly:

"Thank you, Quenella. You were magnificent! Go to sleep now and remember only that you saved the life of a man who was prepared to lose it for India."

As he spoke he left her compartment, closing the door behind him.

Quenella sat down on the edge of her bed.

Had it really all happened? Had what seemed a wild adventure out of some lurid novel really occurred to her?

She had expected many things of her marriage and of India, but not this, and she told herself that the things she had always sensed rather than heard about her uncle should have prepared her.

It was not surprising that he had always spoken of Rex Daviot with a note in his voice which Quenella knew was one of admiration.

Vaguely she remembered hearing that the British had a wonderful counter-espionage system which enabled them to cope with the Russians.

It was obvious to her now that her husband, like the man whose life he had saved, was deeply involved in what was called The Great Game.

Because what had happened had been so exciting while at the same time Rex had behaved in such a practical, calm manner, she was not afraid that it might happen again in the future, but only interested and thrilled to be a part of such an adventure.

She knew, when the man E-Seventeen had fallen at her feet and she had thought he was dead, that she had been struck with a fear that was quite different from the fear she had felt when she had been attacked by the Prince.

'It was more fundamental, more intense,' she analysed to herself.

Then as she got into bed she thought:

'Tomorrow Rex will tell me so much that I want to know.'

As she fell asleep she thought that nothing could be so wonderful as to know that new horizons which she had never dreamt of were opening up in front of her.

Not only was India, with its different religions, its people and its beauty, tugging at her heart, but there was something else which was basically crucial.

It was man pitting his brains against another, and Rex was in the very thick of it.

"I helped him tonight, and I will try to help him again," Quenella promised herself.

* * *

In his own compartment Rex cut into small pieces the dirty clothes he had taken from E-Seventeen.

It would be a great mistake to leave a bundle by the railway-line, because it might be traced to the passing of a particular train on a particular night.

"Never take unnecessary chances," and "Never leave incriminating evidence anywhere," were watchwords which had been beaten into the minds of those who worked in The Great Game.

The pieces of hair were easy to dispose of. He pulled them apart and an hour later as the train gathered speed he opened his window and let them

fly away slowly, not in big bunches but almost a hair
or two at a time.

The towel was easy too. He tore it, soaked it in
water, rubbed the floor with it, and threw it out as any
lazy servant might have done when he thought it was
too much bother to wash it.

Only when some of the things had been disposed of
and the others were waiting until they had gone
farther afield did Rex draw the message from his waist.

He read it carefully, burned it in an ashtray, then
sat down on his bed and wrote out a telegram to a certain small-shop-keeper in Delhi:

*Parcel slightly damaged in transit but received
safely. Send further supplies as previously arranged.*

He added no signature, but told himself that in the
morning his valet would hand it to the Station Master
at the next stop and order it to be despatched immediately.

He then lay down on his bed and shut his eyes.

He was however not thinking of E-Seventeen sleeping peacefully on the platform, nor of those who had
been following him, searching feverishly in the crowds
milling in and out of the station for a man with a
bleeding cheek and a knife-wound in his side.

Instead, he thought of Quenella.

She had done amazingly well in her first encounter
with danger.

Another woman, he thought, and certainly somebody like Kitty Barnstaple, would undoubtedly have
screamed or fainted when a man she thought to be a
native entered her compartment.

Quenella's behaviour was what he would have expected of Sir Terence's niece.

At the same time, she had not lived with her uncle
for long and she had certainly never in her sheltered,

luxurious life encountered anything more dangerous than a Princeling maddened by lust for her beauty.

This was something very different: a man fighting for life itself, who could be saved or destroyed by a woman who screamed at the wrong moment.

"I might have known she would be different," Rex told himself.

Chapter Six

By the time they reached Lucknow, Rex knew that he was in love as he had never before been in love in his whole life.

He had been aware of it first at the moment when standing in Quenella's compartment she had suddenly realised that she was wearing only a transparent lawn nightgown and that he was naked to the waist.

Like her, Rex had been so intent on altering E-Seventeen's appearance and getting him away before the train started that he had not thought of Quenella except as an assistant to do his bidding.

Then when they were alone together and he saw by the expression on her face that she was shy of him as a man, he was vividly aware of her as a woman.

An uncontrollable impulse swept over him to pull her into his arms and kiss her passionately.

He could feel the blood throbbing in his temples and a rising desire swept through him with a razor-like sharpness.

He wanted her so violently at that moment that looking back he knew he had been right when he had first compared her to a tiger-lily.

Beneath her flower-like purity there was a vivid fire which aroused a man to a point where it was impossible for him to think, but only, as the Prince had done, to act.

But because Rex had spent his life controlling himself and hiding his feelings, he had forced a note of indifference into his voice as he said good-night, which he knew left Quenella unafraid.

Lying sleepless for the rest of the night, wanting her in a manner that was the burning desire not only of his body but of his mind, he realised that he was overwhelmingly in love.

It came upon him suddenly, because in her wish to save the wounded man's life Quenella's icy coolness and the barriers of indifference and hatred with which she had surrounded herself had been forgotten.

Instead she had been anxious, sympathetic, compassionate, and of course excited by the drama which had come upon her so unexpectedly.

If he had thought of it, that was what Rex would have wanted in his wife, that she should be courageous, resourceful, and at the same time all woman.

It was as a woman that Quenella aroused him, and both his body and his mind ached and yearned for her.

The next day when they met in the morning in the Sitting-Room between their two bed-rooms, Rex had schooled himself to behave in exactly the same manner as he had before.

He could not help thinking with a faint amusement that of all the many parts he had played, this was going to be the most difficult.

He had thought things out during the night and he had realised that if Quenella was ever to love him, and God knew he wanted her love, he would have to woo her as he had never wooed a woman before.

He knew that in breaking down the first barriers

that existed between them he had only revealed a number of others.

The first step must be for her to trust him, and, he hoped, for her to be intrigued because he was different from any other man she had ever met.

But there was still a very long way to go and he was aware that one hasty word, one uncontrollable gesture, would bring the fear back into her eyes and once again she would withdraw into herself.

He wondered as she came into the central compartment wearing a thin white muslin gown how he had ever imagined for a moment that she did not attract him.

Now he knew it was because she had contrived to disguise her inner self as he had often done when he deceived a thousand savage tribesmen into thinking he was a Fakir, whom they instinctively revered.

He had closed the door to his real self just as Quenella had been able to do.

Now he knew that she was different from any other woman he had ever known and he would fight to win her if it took him a whole lifetime.

Never before had Rex Daviot needed to pursue a woman.

Always they had pursued him and fallen into his arms almost before he was ready to reciprocate.

The mere fact that winning Quenella was going to be as difficult as any part he had ever played in The Great Game was a fascination he was frank enough to admit.

At the same time, he knew that although she was unaware of it, already something spiritual existed between them, and it would be his task to convince her that in their Karmas they belonged to each other.

As she sat down at her usual seat beside the window he saw that there was a light in her eyes and a smile on her lips.

They were alone and after she had glanced over her shoulder she said in a very low voice:

"I have been praying that he got away, but shall we ever hear the end of the story?"

Rex shook his head.

"I am sure he got away, but it is never wise to ask questions."

She gave a little sigh.

"It was all so incredible, and now I shall always be afraid for you."

"For me?"

"I might have been foolish enough not to open the door when he asked me to do so."

Rex understood what she was trying to say, and after a moment he said:

"Let me reassure you by saying that for the moment I have a very different task on my hands as a Lieutenant-Governor. In fact, after what happened last night you may find it rather dull and hum-drum."

"I do not think any life in India could be that," Quenella answered, "but I would like to help and would like also to be part of The Great Game."

Rex smiled at her before he said:

"I am afraid that would be impossible for a woman in your position. Yet sometimes they are able to help, as you did last night."

"Tell me about The Great Game," she said. "I know, now that I have seen how dangerous it is, that it is a typically British name for what it means."

"That is true," Rex replied.

In a low voice he told her of the Anglo-Russian Central Asian rivalry and the espionage which had developed in consequence.

He did not actually tell Quenella anything more than was known by most Senior Officers in the Army and unfortunately by a number of outsiders as well.

At the same time, her imagination made her aware

that the men who were recruited, trained, and initiated into taking their lives in their hands were essential to the protection of India and to the peace of the Eastern World.

Rex had found when he first served on the Northwest Frontier that The Great Game had a network which extended all over India and which involved not only Europeans but a great number of Indians as well.

In a locked book in the Indian Survey Department there was a list of numbers which covered a variety of men and secrets, with which the Russians or other enemies of the country were often rendered powerless or exposed when they least expected it.

It was usual for R-Thirty-two to have no idea of the identity of M-Fourteen, with whom he was in communication, nor did D-Seven have a glimmer of information about G-Twelve.

But sometimes, as last night, in moments of desperate danger there would be somebody to help them, somebody to whom they could appeal as a very last resort.

Rex had no idea how E-Seventeen was aware of his identity. As far as he knew, he had never seen the man before and was unlikely ever to come in contact with him again.

But the fact that he had enlisted his help made him know that in the future he must be more careful than he had been in the past.

Sir Terence had been entirely right to persuade him for the moment to leave the Northwest Frontier and other places where he had operated so successfully.

Rex talked until it was luncheon-time and a servant brought in their meal, which had been supplied at a station where they had halted and where the usual hubbub of noise and commotion took place.

Quenella had risen to walk to the other side of the compartment and raise the Venetian blinds.

She looked out and he knew that she was searching the crowds with a new interest, a new curiosity.

How many of the pushing, shouting people loaded with baggage or crying children were involved in a desperate intrigue that might leave an unknown body dead by the roadside or a man tortured to death for secrets that he would not tell?

She stood half-sideways to him, looking out.

As he saw the soft curves of her breasts, the smallness of her waist, and her perfect, almost Grecian face silhouetted against the kaleidoscope of colour and movement, he felt again the blood rushing to his head, his heart beating frantically in his breast.

Deliberately he forced himself to look out the window beside him, and wondered as he did so how long he would be able to go on acting.

How could he pretend an indifference and an impersonal politeness which he knew he could never feel for her again?

'If I am strong enough to defeat the Russian ambitions and confound their cleverest schemes,' he thought, 'surely I can persuade a young woman to love me?'

But Quenella was not an ordinary young woman!

Then, as always when he was perplexed and unsure of himself, he saw the two golden eagles hovering against the sky at Naini Tal.

He could see them so clearly that it was as if he flew into the sky to join them.

They hovered, then dropped, with the velocity of a bullet and an indescribable grace, into the sunlit valley.

Rex knew then that the power would be given to him.

* * *

They had reached Lucknow and Quenella was entranced by the beauty of the land through which they passed, the fields rich with blue linseed and yellow mustard, backed by acres of sugar-cane.

There were tropical jungles, and marshy alluvial plains below snow-capped mountain ranges.

She loved the curious horizontal lines of smoke near a village at sunset, the cows moving homewards in a cloud of pale gold dust.

Now she saw the city which was to be her home.

Rex had already told her that it had originally been the Capital of the Kings of Oudh and that it was a city where magnificence rubbed shoulders with squalor, a city of pleasure, vice, and intrigue, to which flocked adventurers from all over Asia.

Quenella had therefore expected it to be exciting, but she had not been able to imagine the half of it.

Lucknow was renowned for producing the best roses in India and also the best nautch girls.

But what Quenella saw first was a warren of mudhuts and streets packed with all kinds of humanity, and savage beasts including tethered tigers.

There were also Palaces, Mosques, and Tombs, gimcrack architectural fantasia; and of course the Government buildings on rising ground screened by a girth of trees looked very British.

The original Residency, which had been the centre of a terrible siege during the Mutiny, had been left as it was.

Tattered, roofless, and with a mass of shell-marks where two thousand European women and children who had sheltered there had been killed, it was a ruin which no-one could look at unmoved. It had been left as a monument to British valour.

During the stifling June days of 1857 there were nearly five thousand people within the cramped and exposed area of the compound.

So fierce was the ceaseless cannonade and musket-fire from the surrounding houses that the Residency was really untenable and part of it fell in.

Yet those who survived held out for eighty-seven days against heat, sickness, flies, privation, and enemy attack, until relieved by Sir Henry Havelock on September 25.

After the Mutiny the Chief Commissioner took up residence in a house, in the southeastern part of the city, which was known as Hayat Bakhsh Kothi, or "Life-Giving House"—a somewhat ironic name. It had originally been used as a powder-magazine.

To the British at the time of the Mutiny it was known more simply as Bank's Bungalow.

Because it was in a good position it was merely enlarged and improved by each succeeding Governor.

The thatched roofs had been done away with, the upper storey extended, verandahs added, and by now Bank's Bungalow had become a large, conventional, and attractive Government House.

New kitchens, a Ball-Room, and a *porte-cochère* made it impressive, and Quenella was delighted with the large lofty rooms, the white panelled walls, and the marble floors.

She admired particularly a stone chimney-piece of Oriental design, carved with chrysanthemums, mermaids and fish, which stood in one of the Drawing-Rooms.

But before she had time to inspect the house she and Rex were installed at a ceremony in the Ball-Room. The Chief Justice and other dignitaries of the city were assembled at one end and a Regimental Band was in the Gallery.

They entered to a fanfare of trumpets and Rex took his seat on the gold chair of State.

When the ceremony was over and seventeen guns had thundered deafeningly outside, he and Quenella proceeded down a red carpet to the strains of "The Star of India March," leading the assembled company into an adjoining room where refreshments and champagne were served.

What thrilled Quenella perhaps more than anything else were the gardens.

She had expected that there would be flowers in Lucknow, but not in such profusion, nor so exquisitely beautiful or so breathtakingly colourful.

Later she was to find that the Bazaar, with its saris, gold and silver brocades, pottery, clay figures, and fancy hubble-bubbles, had a fascination that made her go back again and again.

But first the flower-beds filled with fragrant roses and the temple blossoms of the asoka trees scenting the air were too entrancing to leave.

The lawns were weeded and watered by an army of gardeners and the blossoms of the shrubs and trees, almost overwhelming in their profusion, made Quenella wander round feeling that she could never look at them for long enough to appreciate their sheer beauty.

Rex, however, found in the garden something different.

Always in India the Memsahibs planted English flowers which reminded them of home: pansies, asters, phlox, nasturtiums, and marigolds, which did not grow well in India.

They always looked a little sickly, as if it was too much effort to battle against the exuberance of the flowers indigenous to the country.

But still every Englishwoman went on planting, and there were a great number of daisies, asters, and daffodils to be found in the garden at Lucknow, introduced by Lady Hyall, wife of the last Governor, or Lady Cowper before her.

Strangely, amongst them Rex found a cluster of tiger-lilies.

Goodness knows why they had ever been imported from their native land of South America, and they had only reached England in the early 1800s.

But there they were, flamboyant, defiant, exotic, their orange petals spotted with black, reminding him vividly of the tiger-like emotions he had felt when he first met Quenella and what might lay beneath the freezing white untouched snow of her reserve.

Once he had found them he stood looking at them for a long time.

Would he ever arouse Quenella, he wondered, to what Kitty Barnstaple had called so aptly the "fire of love"?

He knew how her mind was turning towards the peaks of knowledge, her instinct towards the inner-most truths which he himself knew were essential to a soul's development.

Yet just as the god Krishna represented the unity of both spiritual and human love, that was what he sought in the woman he loved.

Would the time ever come when they touched the peaks of ecstasy and became both human and Divine?

He was afraid of the answer, and he walked away, but when he returned to the house he ordered some of the tiger-lilies to be picked and placed in a vase on the desk in his office.

Quenella soon realised that it was more difficult to see Rex in Lucknow than she had ever imagined it could be.

When they were in the ship they had been together, and when they travelled in the train she had been able to talk to him.

But at Government House there were always peo-ple to be entertained, Aides-de-Camp in attendance, and so many servants that she had ceased trying to count them.

When they went driving, their carriage was escorted by a squadron of Cavalry and invariably at the end of the drive there was some ceremony in which they had to take part.

She understood that as Rex was the new Governor, everybody of importance must call on him, to be received and entertained.

Yet she suddenly found herself longing for them to be alone together, and when she thought of it she realised that perhaps the only time a Governor and his wife could be together without being disturbed was if they slept in the large white bed which stood in her bed-room.

They at least could talk secretly and intimately as they were unable to do at any other time.

She felt herself blush at the thought and wondered what Rex would say if she asked him to come to her Boudoir after they had both retired for the night.

Of course she only wished to discuss what she had been reading, and perhaps he would go on teaching her the mysteries of the Indian religions as he had done on the voyage from England.

Then she told herself almost despondently that he would not be interested.

She had learnt that every night he worked late in his office at the far end of the house on the ground floor.

There he could be quiet, and although she longed to interrupt him she was far too shy to attempt it.

Every morning an Aide-de-Camp would knock on the door of her private Sitting-Room to show her the programme for the day.

She suddenly had a urge to cross out one of her commitments and put instead:

His Excellency and Lady Daviot will be alone
from five o'clock to seven!

Or better still:

From ten o'clock until midnight!

She could imagine the surprise on the Aide-de-
Camp's face, and she knew she could never risk the
humiliation that Rex might not agree and that those
who served them would be aware of his refusal.

He was always courteous and charming when they
met, and when he complimented her on her appearance or gave her information about those they were
going to meet, she felt that he was interested in her.

She longed to suggest that they should perhaps have
breakfast together before the hurly-burly of the day
started.

But she was sure that if Rex wished to see her he
would have contrived that they should be alone without it seeming strange or in any way unusual.

Then unexpectedly everything changed.

To Quenella's astonishment, although she told herself she had been silly not to anticipate it, she learnt
that in two days' time they were leaving Lucknow, for
Naini Tal, the summer Capital of the Northwest Provinces.

She supposed that she should have realised that
just as the Viceroy left Calcutta for Simla, the Governor of the Northwest Provinces would also have in
the summer a residence somewhere cooler, but it had
never occurred to her.

Rex said casually:

"I think you will enjoy Naini Tal. I know I
am looking forward to being there."

"Naini Tal?" Quenella repeated questioningly.

"We are going there on Wednesday. Did you not know?"

"Nobody told me. Where is it?"

He looked at her in surprise. Then he said:

"I apologise. It was extremely remiss of me to have kept you in ignorance. You must forgive me."

"What am I to forgive?"

"My being so obtuse as not to realise that you did not know that Naini Tal is where the Ruler of this Province lives during the hot weather from the beginning of April."

"Where is it?" she asked.

"It is somewhere which I know will thrill you," he answered, "and which to me is one of the most perfect places in the world."

It was not surprising that Quenella was excited, and when they reached Naini Tal she understood why it appealed to Rex.

It was not until 1839 that the British had discovered a lake hidden amongst the wooded heights of the Himalayan foothills, which according to local legend had grown out of a hole dug by the goddess Naini.

She had, Quenella learnt, forbidden the place to strangers, and when a landslide occurred in 1880, burying the Victoria Hotel, the Assembly Rooms, and the Library, together with a large number of people, the natives all averred that this was her way of punishing an invasion of her privacy.

Sir John Strachey, then Lieutenant-Governor, was unafraid of the goddess's wrath and had built himself a new Government House sited out of reach of landslides, twelve hundred feet above the lake on a lofty summit.

Strangely enough, he had built what was to all intents a Gothic Castle with a row of battlement turrets, some square and some octagonal, in yellow-grey stonework which was gradually covered with creeper-vines.

Government House therefore looked as if it were part of Scotland, and it seemed out-of-place in the middle of the Himalayas, where the mountains and valleys were haunted by a multitude of malign spirits.

Quenella, however, was delighted with the Gothic arches, the top-lit Baronial staircase of dark wood, and the panelling in the Dining-Room relieved only by a few stags' heads.

She loved the log-fires blazing in the huge fire-places because although it was warm in the daytime it was cold at night.

If she had been thrilled with the flowers in Luck-now, they paled into insignificance beside the flowers of Naini Tal.

The compound in which Government House was situated was as large as an English estate, and the flowers grew even in the surrounding forest.

When they arrived, the garden was fragrant with lilies-of-the-valley, the slopes were scarlet with rho-dodendrons, mauve orchids lined the paths, and wild white clematis covered the jungle-shrubs.

What made Quenella breathless with delight were the snow-capped Himalayas rising above Naini Tal, and below, like a stage picture, the plains stretched away for over sixty lovely miles.

Also for the first time since they had arrived in the Northwest Provinces, Quenella could now see some-thing of Rex.

She learnt that there was still entertaining to be done, but to reach them if they gave a dinner, a Ball, or a garden-party, their guests had to make a weary trek up the hill by rickshaw, pony, or *dandy*.

She found it rather amusing, and Rex remarked:

"We are fortunate. In a few years' time I am quite

certain there will be motor cars and people will be bursting in on us when we least want them."

"Motor cars?" Quenella questioned.

She had seen a few cars before they had left England, but somehow she could not imagine them in India.

She could only hope that Rex was not being an accurate prophet.

There was time when the first Receptions were over for her to be alone, and, more important, although she did not exactly admit it to herself, to be with Rex.

"I want to show you something," he said one day.

He led her through the mass of pink and white cosmos which grew near the house, past the great banks of hydrangeas, and into what seemed at first to be almost like a Park in England.

There were oak, beech, and chestnut trees, but their trunks were covered with moss and ferns, and the paths on which they walked were edged with orchids.

"Is the compound very large?" Quenella asked.

"It includes a farm which provides the house with milk, meat, and poultry, and many acres of forest and jungle inhabited by wild deer and panthers!"

They walked for some way, then suddenly Rex came to a halt and Quenella saw in front of her a break in the ground where there had been a landslip.

There was a sheer drop of hundreds of feet, and it seemed fathomless as a small cloud curled below them.

Then she looked up at the stupendous vista of the Himalayas silhouetted against the sky, their peaks encircled by white clouds, the sunshine gleaming golden on the untouched snow.

She could find no words to say how beautiful it was, and Rex beside her said quietly:

"Once when I came here there were two golden

eagles hovering high in the sky. Somehow they became a part of me. Whenever I am in danger or have to make a difficult decision, I think of them."

"And that has . . . helped you?" Quenella asked in a low voice.

"They have told me what to do," he replied, "and they have never been wrong."

He turned to look at her as he spoke. Then he said very quietly:

"I saw them clearly when I was deciding whether or not I would come to meet you at your uncle's invitation."

"They . . . told you to . . . come?"

Quenella did not know why, but it was difficult to speak.

She felt almost as if she were breathless, and there was a strange constriction in her throat.

"They told me it was my fate."

"I wish I had . . . known."

"Why?"

"I think I . . . wasted a lot of time being . . . afraid, and . . . and hating you."

"I understood what you felt."

"I know you . . . did, and it made me . . . angry."

"And now?"

She gave him a sudden smile which seemed to illuminate her face.

"I am . . . glad the eagles told you . . . what to do."

They stood for some time, both looking at the sunshine on the peaks.

It was almost, Rex thought, as if they communicated without words, and he was afraid to break the silence.

Then as they turned to walk back and he thought that there was so much more he wanted to say to her, they saw in the distance coming towards them through the trees an Aide-de-Camp.

"Damn!" Rex swore beneath his breath, and Quenella's heart missed a beat.

She knew that he did not want to be interrupted while they were together.

Somehow the sunshine seemed more golden and she looked back to see if it still illuminated the peaks behind them.

It was dazzling, and she saw with a feeling which she did not quite understand and was afraid to put into words that Rex was scowling at the Aide-de-Camp.

He was being informed that an important caller had arrived who must be received with all due ceremony.

The first day that she had a chance to slip away alone from Government House, Quenella went back to the place where Rex had taken her.

It was after a rather dreary luncheon-party with dull people, and she would have liked to ask Rex to accompany her. But she had learnt before she left that he was in conference and not likely to be free for some time.

She therefore set out alone, carrying a sun-shade and most unconventionally not wearing a hat.

It was delightful to feel that she could be free, un-trammelled by strict protocol and the conventions there had been in Lucknow.

She hummed a little tune to herself as she wandered between the orchids and looked at the white clematis encircling the trees, climbing their trunks with a closeness that had something sensuous about it.

There were also the scarlet flowers of the dhak tree, the famous simal tree, the mauve blossoms of the Bauhinias, and as she moved on through she felt that they were a perfect setting.

"A setting for what?" she asked herself.

Then she knew almost as if she saw him dancing

through the temple blossoms that no place could be more perfect for Krishna, the God of Love.

She had almost reached the spot to which Rex had taken her, when she realised that she was not alone and saw the figure of a man sitting under one of the ancient cedars.

She was not afraid, she was only surprised, for she knew that no-one was allowed inside the Government House compound.

Then she saw it was a Saddhu.

She had seen a number of them by now so she was able to recognise him immediately—the yellow robe thrown carelessly round the body, leaving one shoulder bare, the head shaved in the way Rex had disguised E-Seventeen, and a general air of holiness, of being remote from the world.

Because she was fascinated she moved towards him, stepping off the path on which she had been walking to move between the trees until she stood in front of him.

She saw that he was deep in concentration or prayer and his eyes were closed. She waited, feeling somehow instinctively that he was aware of her presence even though he made no sign of it.

He looked to be a man of fifty. He might indeed have been very much older, for Quenella had learnt that meditation and an aesthetic life, especially amongst the snows, kept a man looking very much younger than his years.

Finally when she had waited for what seemed a long time the Saddhu's eyes opened and he looked at. her.

"Forgive me if I disturb you, Holiness," Quenella said in Urdu, "but I would like to speak to you."

"Speak," the Saddhu replied. "Ask the question which is in your heart."

"The . . . question?" Quenella faltered, taken by surprise. "I am seeking to understand . . . to know so many things."

"You will find what you seek only through love!"

The words came slowly, and yet they were a pronouncement, and as Quenella drew in her breath the Saddhu went on:

"You are looking up at the heights. That is right, but you must also go down into the plains. The two complement each other. That is the law. That is the way to enlightenment."

"I do not . . . think I . . . understand," Quenella replied.

The Saddhu looked at her, his dark eyes seeming, she thought, to look inwards to her innermost soul.

"You understand," he said at length, "and love casts out fear."

He closed his eyes and Quenella knew that their conversation was finished.

For a moment she hesitated. She knew that he had not forgotten her, but he had no more to say and she dared not interrupt him further.

She thought as she moved away that she would think of a hundred questions she wanted to put to him, but instead they did not formulate in her mind. She only found herself remembering what he had said:

"Love casts out fear!"

Strangely, the fears that had beset her when she had left England were gone. They had completely vanished and she was no longer aware of them.

She realised that it was now weeks, perhaps longer, since she had last thought of the Prince.

The hatred and the terror that she had thought would always haunt her had been submerged by the new experiences she had enjoyed in India, and most of all by . . . Rex.

She thought of him not only when he was present

but when she went to bed at night and when she awoke in the morning.

Suddenly she had an urgent desire to be with him, to make him aware of her, to hear his voice.

Because it was an impulse so strong that she could not disobey it, she turned and walked back towards Government House without going on as she had intended to the landslide.

Instead of keeping to the path, she took a direct route through the trees and found before she reached the garden that she had walked into a maze of rhododendrons.

Combined with the white blossoms of the temple flowers, they presented a picture which at any other time would have held her spellbound.

Now she wanted only to reach Rex, and she realised that for the moment she was lost among the shrubs that surrounded the more formal gardens.

She thought she would be wise to go back a little way and find the path with the orchids, but she was impatient and therefore began to push her way through the overgrown shrubs.

Suddenly she heard voices.

Instinctively she paused, and she heard a man say in Urdu:

"Magi will strike anytime now."

It was not only the word "strike" which brought Quenella to a standstill, but it was the way the words were spoken, softly, half a whisper, half a hiss, each syllable slipping over the other.

"How he get in?"

"Amar waiting for him in cellar."

"The guards may see him."

"No, he help Sadhin with logs, sentries foolish, not realise two woodmen, not one."

"That clever!"

"Those who give order clever!"

"That true—and pay well."

There was silence and Quenella held her breath.
Then the first man said:

"How Amar reach Lord Sahib?"

"He there now. Quite easy. Lord Sahib go to office.
When guests gone, fire not lit, Sadhim climb from
cellar into fireplace."

"That clever—very clever!"

"Way prepared two days ago."

"Clever plan—very clever plan!"

The two men chuckled and suddenly Quenella was
aware of the significance of what she had overheard.

It was another move in The Great Game, and Rex
was to be assassinated. But this time the Russians—
who else but the Russians?—had bribed two men em-
ployed at Government House.

Moving slowly so that her presence would not be
revealed, putting each foot down carefully so as not to
snap a twig or draw attention to herself, she crept
away from the rhododendrons.

Moving in the direction which she thought would
take her round them, she sought the path with the
orchids.

It was only when she felt that it was safe to move
quickly that she realised with a sense of panic that she
had lost her way.

Nowhere was there any point she could recognise
and nowhere in fact could she see either the path back
to Government House or the house itself.

There were trees, but covered with white clematis
they all seemed alike. There were rhododendrons and
there appeared to be miles of them, but there was no
way through them.

Frantically she twisted and turned, pushed her
way through the bushes, and all the time she knew
with an ever-rising sense of panic that it was growing
later.

The men, whoever they were, knew, as she did, that Rex would go to his office soon after three o'clock, not much later.

If it was later, the fire would be lit and it would be impossible for Amar to lurk in the great wide fireplace and jump out at him when he was alone.

She had a feeling, although she had not seen the room, that Rex's desk would be in the window, which would mean that the fireplace would be either on his right, his left, or behind him.

How easy for a man to stab or shoot him in the back.

She was certain, however, that because they were in the hill-country the assailant would use a knife, the long, sharp, pointed knife which had accounted for so many deaths of British soldiers, and which they feared as much as bullets.

"Rex! Rex!"

She knew that to save him she must reach him before Amar did, but she was lost—lost in what was now a nightmare of flowers, a hell rather than a Heaven of beauty.

Then suddenly when she felt she must scream for help and hope that somebody would hear her, there was the orchid-edged path and ahead, showing through the trees, the turrets of the house!

Even as she saw it Quenella felt that the sun was not so hot; the shadows were growing and now it was only a question of minutes if she was to save Rex.

Throwing down her sun-shade, she picked up the front of her skirt with both hands and started to run.

She ran faster than she had ever run before, knowing that somehow she must reach the Governor's Office where Rex would be bent over his papers, quite unaware that death lurked beside him.

There was a long corridor which ran the whole

length of the ground floor and Rex's office was at the far end of the west side.

Isolated as it was in Lucknow, the Drawing-Room, the Dining-Room, and the Ball-Room all were at the other end of the house.

Frantically, feeling that there was no time to invoke help, no time to explain to the sentries outside the main door what was occurring, she reached the front door and tore into the Hall, ignoring the servants who stared at her in astonishment.

She knew only too well how difficult it would be to explain the need for her haste and she felt too that they would find her Urdu, spoken in a breathless voice, hard to understand, and the effort of explaining would slow everything.

Instead, turning to the right in the Hall, she ran down the corridor which led to the Governor's Office.

She flung open the door, only to find that the room was empty.

Rex was not there!

For a moment she felt sick with relief, then some sixth sense made her close the door quickly, leaving herself outside in the passage.

If Rex was safe, the man who waited to kill him must be caught and prevented from trying again.

Desperately, with her heart pounding from the rate at which she had run, her lips dry, she tried to think who the two men in the garden were, besides Amar and the man who had helped him reach the cellar.

Even as she stood there trembling, her breath coming through her parted lips, she heard footsteps and saw Rex walking unconcernedly down the passage towards her.

Without thinking, without considering what she should do, only aware that he was safe, alive, and that she could warn him, she ran towards him.

As he looked at her in surprise, she flung herself

into his arms and pressed herself close against him, her cheek against his.

She whispered in a voice he hardly recognised:

"They ... mean to ... kill you! Oh, Rex, there is a ... man waiting to ... kill ... you!"

Wonderingly, Rex's arms went round her, holding her close, and still she whispered against his ear.

"He is ... hidden in the ... fireplace—he has been ... waiting until you are ... alone. ... He has been paid ..."

Rex held her close against him and said quietly:

"It is all right. Do not tremble, but just tell me quietly what has happened."

Because of the terror she had been through, because his arms were so comforting, and because she could not understand the feelings that possessed her, Quenella felt the tears come into her eyes and down her cheeks.

"Do not move," Rex said. "Just tell me slowly and as quietly as you can what you know."

"I got ... lost in the ... garden," she began, "and I ... heard two men ... talking."

"In Urdu?"

"In Urdu ... but I could ... understand."

"Go on!"

"They said someone had paid a man called Amar and he would get into the house with Sadhin when he carried in the logs. He was to ... hide in the cellar and climb up into ... your office through the ... fireplace. A hole was ... prepared two ... days ago!"

She paused because it was so hard to breathe, and Rex said against her ear:

"Go on! Take your time."

"He will ... kill you ... I think with a knife ... while you are at your desk ... and ... I was terrified I would be ... too late!"

"But you are not," he said quietly. "Now listen: go

to the Aides-de-Camp's room and tell whoever is there to send two soldiers immediately to guard the door into the cellar."

He stopped speaking and Quenella moved her head to look at him.

"And send other . . . soldiers here?"

"Later," Rex agreed, "when I ask for them."

Her eyes widened and she cried:

"You are not . . . going in there . . . alone?"

"I shall be all right."

"No! No!"

Her arms tightened round his neck.

"I cannot . . . bear it . . . he will kill you—please, Rex, let the soldiers go . . . not you!"

"I shall be more effective than the soldiers!"

"I may . . . be wrong . . . he might have a . . . revolver."

"I can take care of myself."

"You are . . . walking into danger. . . . They want to . . . kill you, and if they do . . . I could not . . . bear it!"

She felt his arms tighten round her as she spoke. Then he said:

"Trust me."

"Please . . . please be more . . . careful."

"I will be because you ask me," he answered.

Then, as she stared up at him, her eyes filled with tears, pleading with him not only with words but with every nerve in her body, he looked down at her.

Then as if he could not help himself his lips touched hers.

It was only for a second. Then she was free, and as he released her he said in a very different tone:

"Go to the Aides-de-Camp's room as I told you!"

It was an order and he was moving away.

She wanted to cling on to him and beg him even on

her knees not to do anything so foolish, so dangerous, as to go into his office alone.

But she knew that he would not listen, and she turned away despairingly to carry out his orders, knowing that she loved him and if she lost him now, everything that mattered would have gone out of her life.

Chapter Seven

As he left Quenella, Rex walked slowly and un-hurriedly towards his office.

He opened the door, stepped inside the room, and stood still for a moment. Then he said aloud in an irritated tone:

"Damn!"

He walked to the door and slammed it, but he re-mained inside the room.

For a moment he was very still, taking his bearings.

Quenella had been right in thinking that his desk was in front of the window and the fireplace was to his left.

He anticipated that whoever was waiting for him would be in the left-hand corner, as from there it was possible to see him at the desk.

The room was quite a large one, and after a mo-ment's silence he began to walk noiselessly along the wall which it was impossible to see from that corner of the fireplace.

One of the first things those in The Great Game were taught was to move without being heard.

This of course was particularly easy for Indians,

who went bare-footed, but far more difficult for Englishmen, who wore shoes or boots.

Fortunately Rex had mastered the art of moving without making a sound in whatever he wore, and after a few seconds he reached the side of the protruding marble chimney-piece.

He drew from his pocket slowly and without haste a small coin and sent it spinning to the far corner of the room.

It was an old trick, but it worked.

The man waiting in the shadows of the fireplace stretched out his neck to see what the noise could be, and the next moment a pincer-like hand gripped him agonisingly by the neck while an excruciating pain in his right wrist caused him to drop the sharp-pointed knife he held.

* * *

Quenella reached the Aides-de-Camp's room and burst in to find that its only occupant was Captain Anderson, who was in the same Regiment as Rex.

He was reading, and if she had not been so agitated Quenella would have been interested to notice that it was a book on Tibet.

As she stood in the doorway, her breath coming quickly, the tears still on her cheeks, Captain Anderson after one startled glance rose to his feet.

"Your Excellency. . . !" he began.

"You are to send . . . two soldiers to the door of the . . . cellar, and let . . . no-one escape," Quenella said. "Hurry! Hurry! There is no . . . time to lose!"

Captain Anderson did not ask questions, he merely obeyed the order, which he knew had come from the Governor.

Rex had chosen his Aides-de-Camp well.

Captain Anderson passed Quenella quickly and she

leant against the lintel of the door, feeling curiously weak, and yet at the same time every nerve in her body was tense because Rex was in danger.

How could she know, how could she ever have guessed, that love would make her feel an agony of fear that was quite different from anything she had felt about herself?

Becaause she was so apprehensive she wanted to fetch the sentries from the front door and scream for the assistance of the servants.

But she knew, like Captain Anderson, that she had her orders and the one thing she must not do was disobey them.

Slowly, with feet which felt as though they could hardly carry her, she walked back down the long passage the way she had come.

She approached Rex's office, listening, feeling as if every other sound in the house was constituting a barrier against the voice she most wanted to hear.

Silence would be ominous, for dead men do not speak.

Then when she felt in a panic-stricken manner that everything was quiet and she was sure that Rex was lying bleeding to death from a knife-thrust, she heard his voice.

She could not hear what he said but she recognised his calm tone, and because it was such a relief once again the tears ran down her cheeks.

He went on speaking and occasionally another voice joined his in the whining tones, she thought, of a man pleading for mercy.

"Why does he not kill him?" she asked angrily, then was shocked at herself that she should be so bloodthirsty.

But if it was a matter of Rex's life or another man's, she knew there was no question of choice.

One man or a thousand—they could all die as long as Rex lived.

A few minutes later she heard Captain Anderson's footsteps as he came to join her, and as he did so Rex opened the door of his office.

He stood there silhouetted against the light and everything that Quenella had wanted to say died on her lips.

She could only stare at him as if he were an apparition from out of the sky, Heaven-sent to take away her fear.

"Come in, Anderson!" Rex said to the Aide-de-Camp, and when Captain Anderson moved forward, Quenella followed him into the room.

On the floor was a miserable creature, his hands bound with his own turban, a handkerchief gagging him, preventing him from making any further sound.

Rex made a gesture towards him.

"Have this man taken away and locked up," he said. "He will be charged with theft, as will the woodman whom you will find in the cellar. Two gardeners, Daud and Hari, are to be arrested and will also be charged with conspiring to steal. They are to have no communication with one another."

"I understand, Your Excellency," Captain Anderson said.

"Keep their detention as quiet as possible," Rex went on. "And order two horses to be brought to the side-door. I will take Azim with me."

Quenella stared at Rex in amazement.

She knew that Azim was his personal servant, a man who had been with him for many years.

Where was he going, and why with Azim?

The question trembled on her lips as Captain Anderson, after a quick glance at the man lying on the floor, to see that he was securely tied, turned and walked away down the corridor.

Now Rex looked at her with a smile on his lips.

She would have spoken, but he drew her out of the office, shutting the door behind him.

"Where are you . . . going? And why do you need a . . . horse?" she began, and he interrupted:

"I will be as quick as I can, but I may be late for dinner. I leave you to carry on until I return. No-one must have any idea that I am not in the house."

"Rex! Rex!" Quenella cried frantically.

"I told you to trust me, as I trust you," he said. "You wished to play a part in The Great Game."

She wanted to protest: "Not like this!" not knowing anything, and feeling that he was going again into danger and she was to be left behind.

But before she could formulate even one sentence he was gone, walking down the corridor.

He turned into a room that was not in use but which led, she was aware, to another staircase, which would take him up to his own bed-room without being observed.

For a moment she felt that it was too much to be borne.

She could not do what he asked of her, but must run after him and beg him to take her with him or to tell her more.

To be left in doubt, in fear and anxiety that was like a knife cutting into her, was beyond human endurance.

Then she remembered that Rex trusted her, and because she could not let him down she walked slowly and with dignity into the main Hall and up the staircase to her own Sitting-Room.

There was no-one about and no sign of Rex outside the Suite which was always occupied by the Lieutenant-Governor and his wife.

It consisted of a large bed-room, which she used herself, cool and white, with three windows looking out over the garden and the beautiful view of the mountains beyond.

Her Sitting-Room, which was filled with flowers, was next door and communicated with the Governor's bedroom, which she had never seen.

Quenella sat down for a moment, then rose to stand at the window, seeing nothing of the beauty that had enthralled her ever since she had come to Naini Tal but only Rex riding unescorted into danger.

She knew without being told that he had gone to find the man who had been instrumental in setting up the plot to kill him.

The man who she suspected was either a Russian or in their pay, and to whom Rex's dead body would be a moral as well as a physical victory.

The agony of her thoughts made her put her hands up to her face and as she suffered she thought of how she had prayed to Lord Krishna to bring her love.

She had not known then that love could be a two-edged weapon.

It was not, as she had believed, an ecstasy of the mind raised to the shining peaks, but something quite different.

Now she really understood what the Saddhu had meant when he had said:

"You must also go down into the plains."

That was where she was now. Distraught and torn by human suffering, by human emotions, by love that was not ecstatic but something much more fundamental.

She felt herself shaking with the intensity of what she felt. Then she could hear Rex's voice, calm, quiet, and yet commanding:

"Trust me, as I trust you."

* * *

A Pathan travelling in a rickshaw which he had picked up on the edge of the town of Naini Tal walked in through the door of a dingy Lodging-House.

Beneath the dusty-layered blue turban were the eyes of a hawk, and his long, unwashed white robe was worn over a pair of ankle-length pants and a dirt-caked tunic festooned with charms and armlets.

He moved with the silent grace of a panther on the stalk.

The Pathan's cotton cummerbund held his trousers and tunic in place and was also the repository for an oversized flint-lock pistol, two knives, and a long, carved *tulwar* that could mince a floating feather.

Two red roses were behind his ears and did nothing to dispel the impression that the Pathan's sole purpose and pleasure in life was the inflicting of death—both painful and prolonged.

He walked up to the proprietor of the Lodging-House, a fat, lazy Babu who had invested his life-savings in the sleezy building, and asked in a queer, guttural voice:

"Which room I find foreign Sahib?"

The Babu looked up suspiciously. At the same time, he was acutely aware of the knives and the *tulwar*.

"He expect you?" he asked.

The Pathan made an almost imperceptible gesture with his head and the Babu pointed to the rickety wooden stairs.

"Number two."

The Pathan looked round the small, dirty hall, then climbed the stairs in the swaggering manner that was characteristic of his race.

After ten decades of association with the Pathans, the British could never quite make up their minds about them.

"Ruthless, cowardly robbers, cold-blooded, treacherous murderers," wrote one officer from the Frontier.

"Nothing can ever change these shameless, cruel savages."

But another saw the tribesmen differently:

"The Pathan is brave, sober, religious according to his lights, has a ready sense of humour, and is a lover of sport."

Whatever the Babu's opinion of the visitor to his Lodging-House, he was not prepared to express it or to argue with the man who had just gone upstairs.

The Pathan entered bed-room number two without knocking.

Lying on the bed was the type of foreigner he expected, a man who was obviously better-educated than his appearance suggested, and whose features indicated that did not belong to India or to Afghanistan.

His clothes were deliberately chosen to make him appear the tourist he pretended to be.

Lying on a table were a few canvasses and a paint-box. It was an old excuse for wandering round the foothills of the Himalayas, and the word "artist" could cover a multitude of other interests.

The Pathan shut the door behind him and the man on the bed sat up.

It was all over very quickly and it was not until the following morning that the Babu, anxious as to why his guest had not demanded anything to eat, entered the bed-room to find the foreign Sahib had suffered a "heart-attack" and was lying dead on his bed.

There were no marks of violence on his body nor was there any sign of the Pathan, who had certainly not left the Lodging-House by the staircase to the hall.

But then the first floor of a low building is not very far from the ground!

* * *

Quenella could never remember afterwards what

she had said to the guests who had arrived and had
been presented to her by Captain Anderson.

Naini Tal, she had learnt, had a reputation for luxurious living; the sweet-meats which were served before dinner were certainly delicious, and their guests
seemed to enjoy the wine.

She had dressed as if in a dream, letting her maid
choose the gown that she should wear and the jewels
which were fastened round her neck and arranged in
her hair.

She could only stare blindly into the mirror, seeing
not her own face but Rex's.

His lips had touched hers, but she felt that it was
only the reassuring gesture he might have given a
child.

She wanted much more from his lips and from ...
him.

In the Drawing-Room she found it almost impossible
to concentrate on what was being said, and yet because
the guests were laughing and apparently at ease, she
knew that she was behaving automatically in the manner that would be expected of her.

She tried to prevent herself from looking every
other second at the large ormolu clock which stood on
the mantelpiece.

Was it possible that time could move so slowly?

She knew that dinner was already a quarter-of-an-
hour late. Still the Khidmatgars, in white, scarlet, and
gold, continued to fill up the glasses.

She made no move to lead the way into the Dining-
Room, where the long table, with its damask cloth, its
display of glittering plate, and its napkins cunningly
folded to resemble fans or exotic birds, was ready to
receive them.

"Rex! Rex!"

Quenella felt her heart calling out to him.

What could have happened? Why did he not come?

How could she have let him leave without knowing where he was going or what he intended to do?

She felt as if there was a heavy stone in her breast, growing larger and larger until it prevented her from breathing.

Suddenly a Khidmatgar flung open the door and Rex was there, conventionally dressed, be-medalled, and smiling!

Everyone rose to their feet and the ladies curtseyed while the men bowed.

Quenella felt as if the lights had all suddenly flared like torches into the sky and the room was lit with a brilliance that was almost blinding.

For a moment Rex's eyes met hers and she knew that all was well.

Then, when the guests had been presented to him, he offered her his arm and they led the way in to dinner.

The Khidmatgars, one for each guest, drawn up in a line, saluted as was the custom in the Government House of the Northwestern Province.

Rex did not speak, but he put his hand for one moment over hers as it lay on his arm, and she thrilled at his touch.

After that, Quenella felt that she was being very witty and her conversation was unusually intelligent, for everyone to whom she spoke appeared to be laughing.

After Rex's arrival the tempo rose, and she thought as the evening ended that it was in fact, although she could not remember one word that had been said, the best dinner-party they had ever given.

She and Rex went up the stairs side by side in silence, and only when they reached their Suite did she say quickly, for fear that he was about to say goodnight:

"I . . . must know . . . you must . . . tell me."

"Will you allow me first to take off my finery?" he asked. "And I am sure you would be more comfortable without yours."

"Yes . . . of course," she agreed.

She went into her room and he went into his.

Her maid was waiting, a Bengali who had been specially chosen for her in Calcutta, having served other Governors' wives, and, as was written on her reference, "well up in her duties."

She undid Quenella's gown and put away her jewels.

"Shall I brush your hair, Your Excellency?" she enquired.

"No, not tonight," Quenella answered.

The maid brought from the wardrobe a wrap which was of white lined satin trimmed with lace and small velvet bows of blue ribbon.

Quenella put it on.

"You may go now, Nalini," she said. "I will get into bed later."

The maid dimmed the lights except for those by the bed-side, then went from the room.

Quenella knelt down on the thick white fur rug in front of the fire.

The logs were piled high and the flames leapt above them.

'In this room at least,' she thought, 'no-one could hide in the chimney.'

However, for the moment she was not afraid.

She was only waiting, while her heart was beating frantically in her breast and her lips felt dry.

Then the door opened and Rex came in. He was wearing a long, very English-looking dressing-gown, which, with its frogged braid across the front, made him look as if he were still fully dressed.

He walked towards her and she sprang to her feet. Even before he reached her she asked:

"You . . . are all . . . right? You are not . . . hurt?"

He smiled at the question.

"As you see, I have returned to you intact, as I intended to do."

"And the ... man? You found ... him?"

"I found him!"

"What ... happened?"

"Is it important?" he asked.

Her eyes met his and it was difficult to think of anything else but the expression in the grey depths of them.

He came a little nearer.

"You saved my life, Quenella, and I think I should first thank you for it."

"It was chance ... pure chance," she said. "Supposing I had not ... lost my way? Suppose I had not ... overheard the gardeners ... talking?"

"Was it chance that threw us together?" Rex asked. "Chance that we should be married, chance that you should be exactly the type of wife for whom, although I did not realise it, I had always been seeking?"

She looked at him wide-eyed.

"Is ... that true?"

"Do you think I could tell you anything that was not true without you being aware of it?"

For a moment they looked at each other. Then Rex said:

"There is so much we have to say to each other, but first I want to thank you not only for saving me but for the tears you had in your eyes when I left you."

Because there was something very soft and gentle in his voice, and yet with an undercurrent of a deeper emotion, Quenella felt herself trembling, and her eyelashes were dark against her cheeks.

"I am afraid," Rex said unexpectedly.

"Afraid?" she questioned, surprised at the word.

"Of frightening you if I tell you what is in my heart."

"You . . . need not be . . . afraid."

"You are certain of that?"

She was not sure whether she took a step towards him or whether his arms drew her there. She only knew that she was close against him, and she thought he must feel the wild throbbing of her breasts.

"I touched your lips in gratitude," Rex said in a very deep voice, "but now I want to kiss you for another reason."

"What is . . . that?"

It was almost impossible to speak as she raised her face to his.

She thought he would kiss her, but instead he ran his fingers along the outline of her chin and upwards to touch her ear, then downwards to the round column of her neck.

It gave her a sensation she had never known, tingling, like flames through her body, which made her lips part so that the breath could come fitfully through them.

"You are so beautiful!" he said. "But it is not only your face that excites me."

"I . . . excite you?"

She had to hear the answer.

"More than I dare tell you," he replied. "It has nearly driven me insane these past weeks not to touch you, not to hold you like this."

"I wanted you . . . to."

The words burst from her; then, because she had to be honest, she added:

"B-but I did not . . . realise it until today . . . when I thought . . . you would be killed . . . and I could not . . . warn you in . . . time."

There was so much pain in the way she spoke that Rex knew how she had suffered, and he pulled her closer against him.

Just for a moment he looked down into her eyes, then his lips were on hers.

As he touched them he found that the fire was there beneath the snow, burning with a fierceness and a violence that consumed everything but their need for each other.

They were reunited, they had met after centuries of time, but as the flames leapt higher and higher it was impossible to think, but only to feel. . . .

* * *

A long time later, when the logs in the fireplace were smouldering into ashes, Quenella said:

"I thought . . . that I would . . . never be alone with you . . . because there were always . . . people with us, and I was . . . envious of the other Governors and their wives who were . . . able to be alone together in . . . this bed."

Rex's lips were against her forehead as he answered:

"That at least is something which we will share in the future, and I think, my precious love, that we are both entitled to more than that."

"Wh-what do you . . . mean?"

"When we were in England we were promised a honeymoon in Lucknow. I think we are entitled to take one in Naini Tal."

"A . . . honeymoon?"

The question was hardly audible, and yet there was a lilt behind it.

"Is that what you would like?"

"I would adore . . . anything which meant I could be with you . . . so that I could . . . talk to you . . . so that you could . . . love me."

There was a little quiver in the last words, which were echoed by the movement of her body against his.

"We have wasted too much time," Rex said, "and now I intend to have my wife to myself."

"Will they . . . let you?" Quenella asked.

"They? Who are 'they'?" Rex enquired. "Am I or am I not the Governor of this Province and answerable for the moment to no man but myself?"

She gave a little laugh.

"Then perhaps, Your Excellency, you will . . . tell me what you . . . intend we shall do?"

"It is very regrettable," Rex said slowly, "but we shall both for the next two weeks be suffering from a spring fever which will prevent us from carrying out any official duties!"

Quenella snuggled a little closer to him.

"And is it a . . . fever which feels like little . . . flames flickering . . . inside one?"

"Exactly!"

"And does it give those who . . . have it a . . . strange constriction in the . . . throat, which makes it . . . hard to speak above a . . . whisper?"

"It does!" Rex agreed.

"And do their . . . eye-lids feel heavy . . . and their lips a little swollen?"

"An inescapable symptom! What else do I make you feel?"

"So much . . . much . . . more!"

Quenella's voice faltered as she went on:

"I felt you lifted me up to the mountain-peaks where . . . no-one has ever been before, and there were . . . only the gods."

She was silent and then she asked tentatively:

"Did . . . you feel . . . anything like that?"

"For me, my lovely one," Rex answered, "our love was an ecstasy beyond words, and I have never—this is true—felt so happy, so fulfilled."

"Oh, I am glad . . . so very . . . very . . . glad!"

"It can all be summed up in one word—*love!*"

"I love you! I love you!"

"You are quite certain I have not hurt or frightened you?" he asked. "I meant, my precious darling, to be very gentle, to woo you very slowly so that you would never be afraid."

"I was not . . . afraid," Quenella answered, "but I did not know that one could be utterly consumed in a fire and it would be the most perfect . . . the most marvellous thing that could ever . . . happen!"

"The fire of love!"

"That is what it . . . was like."

He swept her hair back from her face and looked down at her, and in the last dying light from the logs he saw her eyes looking up at him and her lips inviting his.

"I have so much to teach you, my beautiful flower, and there is so much for you to teach me," he said.

"About . . . what?"

"About our souls, our spirits, and our bodies," he answered. "We have both been struggling alone. Now there is the joy of thinking and feeling the same, of finding our way together up to the highest peak."

"You said it was . . . possible to achieve the . . . impossible," Quenella murmured, "and you were . . . right."

Rex took the last word from her lips with his, and only when he had kissed her until she was breathless, until her heart was beating as frantically as his, did he say:

"I must let you sleep, my darling. We are leaving quite early tomorrow, and we will be riding."

"Where are we going?"

"There are many places I wish to show you, holy places, places which are not known to the ordinary visitors to Naini Tal."

"I shall love that."

"They can only be reached on horseback."

"Can we really go alone?"

"If you are prepared to risk meeting the spirits and the gods who live in the mountains, then I promise you there will be no need for any escort."

Quenella gave a little sigh of sheer happiness.

"Oh, Rex, I never thought anything so... wonderful could be... waiting for me... but I would not have you risk being in... danger, even to make me ... happy."

"You are thinking of me?"

"Who else?" she asked. "There is no-one else. You fill the whole world, the sky, the mountains, and... the plains."

She hesitated on the last words, and Rex asked:

"Why did you say 'plains' like that?"

"Because of what the Saddhu said to me."

"What Saddhu?"

"He was sitting in the compound and he told me that I was looking for the... heights but that I must also go... down into the... plains."

She hesitated for a moment, then she said:

"I think he ... meant by the ... plains, the fire and sensations you have just given me."

"That is what I thought."

"The Saddhu said that the heights and the plains ... complemented each other and that that was the ... way to enlightenment."

"Which we will find together."

"Oh, darling, darling Rex!" Quenella said passionately. "How could I have believed when I left England that this would happen to me?"

"It has happened!" he answered. "And this is only the beginning. We have much more to do together."

He was about to kiss her but she hid her face as she asked:

"There is ... something ... I want to say to you."

"What is it?"

He knew she was seeking for words, and he waited, thinking he had never known that such happiness existed.

Quenella's voice was like the music as she said:

"The books you gave me said that Hindu girls ... worship their husbands because each ... believes her husband to be ... Krishna, the ... God of Love."

"That is true."

"And ..." Quenella whispered, "the ... act of love ... is therefore ... Divine."

Rex did not speak, and she went on:

"That is what ... I felt! To me you are ... Krishna, the love you ... gave me was ... holy, and ... I worship ... you."

He held her so close that she could not breathe.

"My darling, my precious, wonderful wife, you must not say such things. It is I who must worship you, because you are perfect."

She put up her arms in an impulsive gesture and pulled his head down to hers, her lips seeking his, her body pressed against him.

Then the fire within them burst into flames and, rising higher and higher, burning wildly and passionately with the violence of love, carried them up towards the peaks of ecstasy. . . .

* * *

It was early in the morning and the sun was not over-hot as Rex lifted Quenella onto the saddle of the horse waiting outside the front door.

Captain Anderson saw them off.

"The servants are to bring out the luncheon on packhorses and lay it under the trees above the Naini Cascade," Rex ordered. "They are to be there at noon, then move out of sight, and collect what is left two hours later."

Quenella made a little sound of delight but she did not interrupt.

"I will see that it is done," Captain Anderson replied.

"And make it quite clear that there will be no official engagements for two weeks," Rex went on. "You can deal with anything that is urgent."

The Aide-de-Camp hesitated for a moment, then he asked:

"If I am doubtful about anything in particular, may I discuss it with Your Excellency this evening?"

"No!" Rex said firmly. "We will dine in Her Excellency's Sitting-Room, with only Azim to wait on us. As far as the household is concerned, we are not in residence. There are no exceptions to the rule!"

"Very good, Your Excellency."

Then Captain Anderson smiled and added:

"Good luck, My Lord, and may I offer my somewhat belated but very sincere congratulations!"

"Thank you, Anderson."

Rex turned to mount his own horse. As he did so, one of the gardeners came towards the house.

He carried on one arm a huge basket of freshly cut roses and in his other hand there was a bunch of tiger-lilies.

"Give me those!" Rex said, taking them from him.

He swung himself onto his horse and fixed the lilies to the front of his saddle.

Then he and Quenella rode away, Captain Anderson and the two sentries outside the front door saluting as they went.

Only when they reached the orchid-lined paths which led through the Park did Quenella ask curiously:

"Why did you want the tiger-lilies?"

"Because they are the flower I have always identified with you," Rex answered. "To me they symbolise purity and at the same time the wildness of the tiger."

She understood what he was trying to say, and she blushed.

"But what are you . . . going to do with . . . them?" she enquired after a moment.

Rex looked up at the snow-capped mountains that were discernible through the blossom-covered branches of the trees, then at Quenella.

"I intend," he said, "to lay them on the first Shrine we find dedicated to the God of Love!"

Their eyes met. She looked very desirable against the background of white, scarlet, and blue blossoms.

"I prayed that Lord Krishna would give me love," Quenella said softly. "How can I thank Him?"

"We have, my darling, all eternity in which to do so," Rex answered.

ABOUT THE AUTHOR

BARBARA CARTLAND, the world's most famous romantic novelist, who is also an historian, playwright, lecturer, political speaker and television personality, has now written over 200 books.

She has also had many historical works published and has written four autobiographies as well as the biographies of her mother and that of her brother Ronald Cartland, who was the first Member of Parliament to be killed in the last war. This book has a preface by Sir Winston Churchill.

Barbara Cartland has sold 100 million books over the world, more than half of these in the U.S.A. She broke the world record in 1975 by writing twenty books, and her own record in 1976 with twenty-one. In addition, her album of love songs has just been published, sung with the Royal Philharmonic Orchestra.

In private life, Barbara Cartland, who is a Dame of the Order of St. John of Jerusalem, has fought for better conditions and salaries for Midwives and Nurses. As President of the Royal College of Midwives (Hertfordshire Branch), she has been invested with the first Badge of Office ever given in Great Britain, which was subscribed to by the Midwives themselves. She has also championed the cause for old people and founded the first Romany Gypsy Camp in the world.

Barbara Cartland is deeply interested in Vitamin Therapy and is President of the British National Association for Health.

Barbara Cartland

The world's bestselling author of romantic fiction. Her stories are always captivating tales of intrigue, adventure and love.